TOE TAGZ

Ah'Million

Lock Down Publications and Ca$h
Presents
Toe Tagz
A Novel by *Ah'Million*

Ah'Million

Lock Down Publications
P.O. Box 870494
Mesquite, Tx 75187

Visit our website @
www.lockdownpublications.com

Copyright 2019 by Ah'Million
Toe Tagz

First Edition December 2019
Printed in the United States of America

Lock Down Publications
Like our page on Facebook: Lock Down Publications @
www.facebook.com/lockdownpublications.ldp
Cover design and layout by: **Dynasty Cover Me**
Book interior design by: **Shawn Walker**
Edited by**: Sunny Giovanni**

Stay Connected with Us!

Text **LOCKDOWN** to 22828 to stay up-to-date with new releases, sneak peaks, contests and more...

Thank you.

Submission Guideline.

Submit the first three chapters of your completed manuscript to ldpsubmissions@gmail.com, subject line: Your book's title. The manuscript must be in a .doc file and sent as an attachment. Document should be in Times New Roman, double spaced and in size 12 font. Also, provide your synopsis and full contact information. If sending multiple submissions, they must each be in a separate email.

Have a story but no way to send it electronically? You can still submit to LDP/Ca$h Presents. Send in the first three chapters, written or typed, of your completed manuscript to:

LDP: Submissions Dept
Po Box 870494
Mesquite, Tx 75187

DO NOT send original manuscript. Must be a duplicate.

Provide your synopsis and a cover letter containing your full contact information.

Thanks for considering LDP and Ca$h Presents.

Acknowledgement

First and foremost, I would like to thank God. All glory goes to him. I would also like to thank my brothers who gave me the motivation and encouragement to use my dream. Secondly, my mother. Her daily struggle made me strive to go harder. This is for my Uncle "Lil Boy". Since I was young, he told me I was going to be someone important in life. I love you Suga Momma. Last but not least I would like to thank my best friend/other half who was there every step of the way. Ha! Ha! To my haters who thought I wouldn't make it past the walls! To my friends and family, free and on lock, I love you all. Enjoy.

Ah'Million

CHAPTER I
WELCOME HOME

Feeling like I'm bulletproof. Bang! Bang! Bang! Yo Gotti blasted from the speakers, as Mun and Rico navigated through the streets of Dallas, Texas.

"Turn that down real quick," Mun shouted over the loud music to Rico in the passenger seat.

When Rico turned the volume down Mun called his older sister Quaylo. As soon as she answered, he said, "I'm coming down your street, so be ready."

"Okay."

Though, she could afford to live anywhere in the city, Quaylo preferred to live in the slums of East Dallas. She was the type of female who got it out the mud, the ski mask way, so the hood was right up her alley.

Twenty minutes later, she was walking up to her brother's black on black Magnum looking delicious. She stood 5'6 and weighed 160 lbs, but her weight was distributed well. Quaylo had a cocoa brown complexion, shoulder length dreads, almond-shaped brown eyes, and a deep, sexy dimple in her left cheek. Her smile was enhanced by two gold slugs that accentuated her pretty, white teeth.

She climbed in the backseat, feeling exuberant. "What's up niggas?" she spoke.

"You know what today is. You ready?"

"Hell yeah, I'm ready. It's been a long time coming. I miss my nigga. Shit ain't been the same without him!" She answered in a chipper voice.

They headed to the Greyhound down South to pick up the youngest brother, Donk. He'd just gotten through a six-year bid for robbing a jewelry store back in 2009. He was the most ruthless out of the three. He would shoot, kill, and rob with no remorse. As Mun cruised down I-10 he glanced at Qualyo through his rearview mirror who was exchanging seductive glances with Rico. *Must be the Kush*, he thought as he quickly shook it from his mind and diverted his attention ahead of him.

Rico was handsome, light skinned and muscle-toned with hazel eyes. The nigga was so fine, being in his presence alone would make your panties wet, and his swag was so official that when he walked into a room you could see the confidence in his stride. His attitude was charming but ruthless. Even at a young age he always had a hustle. The only difference is he was no longer in elementary, stealing candy from convenience stores and selling it, busting them down.

Mun came to a stop on the side of the curb in front of the Greyhound station. "I guess we wait," he suggested, looking around curiously. Minutes passed and still no sign of Donk. He sat and observed the other men as they greeted their families. A smile slowly formed across his face when he saw Donk stepping off the bus. He waited to get his attention, wanting to see his reaction firsthand.

Donk looked around curiously but annoyed.

"Donk!" Mun shouted, waving his hand in the air.

Donk immediately started glowing as he sprinted toward the car.

"My nigga!" Mun yelled, pulling Donk into a tight hug.

"Damn, nigga, you big!" Quaylo screamed as she walked to the other side of the car and wrapped her arms around Donk's neck.

"I missed y'all too, fam. It's been a minute but it's all good, 'cause it ain't no going back." Donk assured as he walked around to her side of the car.

Rico opened the passenger door before Donk could reach for the handle. "Wassup, bro?" Rico was ecstatic.

"Wassup?" Donk replied dryly. He had never been fond of Rico, despite his good deeds. He just felt Rico always tried to take his place.

"Aye, sit back there with Quay. Me and Donk got a lot of catching up to do." Mun stated.

10

Rico wanted to say something but decided against it and climbed into the backseat with Quaylo.

Donk remained cool after he picked up on Rico's uneasiness about having to get in the back. He quickly brushed it off, realizing he'd have to be level headed if he was Mun right hand man. Mun and Donk laughed and reminisced on the ride back to Dallas. Quaylo and Rico must have been in a deep conversation, because neither one of them heard Mun.

"Aye!" Mun snapped, his face suddenly serious. They both jumped and looked at him. "Damn, what y'all jump for? What y'all want to eat?" Mun asked annoyed.

"Shit, whatever Donk want." Quaylo replied jolly.

"Fuck it, let's go to the hood store!" Donk shouted, grinning at Mun as they sped through the light. *It feel so good to finally be free*, Donk thought.

Mun pulled up at the hood store. Donk realized nothing had changed but the dates on his calendar. The thots were still bopping, pushers still pushing, and the jack boys were still on the lurk. Mun couldn't even park his car without people shouting his name and walking up to the car.

"Ooohhh, shit, it's Donk!"

"Wassup, nigga!"

"We missed you, boy!"

Different voices called out. Donk loved every minute of the attention he was getting. He hopped out the Magnum, dapped up all his hood niggas and gave hugs and winks to the bitches. He strolled into the store with a few of his potnas on his trail.

"Aye, let me get a cheeseburger, mayo and mustard; everything except pickles; a large fry, large onion ring, and a six-piece chicken tender with extra honey mustard," Donk ordered. He's really grown over the years. He stood at 6'3", broad shoulders, chiseled structured face, with the body of a king. His high cheek bones were really the charm. In the joint he kept his hair in a college cut, but he really liked to rock a bald fade. He had a smile that turned heads. Maybe it was his two gold slugs with princess cut diamonds. Donk was surpassingly sluggish and mysterious.

His beady, dark brown eyes were phlegmatic and distinct, and his blank expression would send chills down your spine. His aura was demanding and powerful, yet his smile was sexy and alluring. It made him irresistible at twenty-one years old. He was the youngest and the coldest.

"Mention my name, bring the whole city out." Mun chanted as he walked into the store and shook hands with Donk again, barely being able to contain his excitement. With Donk being home, a lot of shit was subject to change.

"Bro, it's good to be home." Donk said looking around the store, treasuring the little things; even the dust bunnies that hid in between the crevices of the wall.

"I know you know I got some shit set up for you."

"That's wassup, but you know I ain't no trap nigga. I like taking shit from niggas who don't deserve it."

"You still on that jack boy shit. You got to be careful, nigga, but you know I'm gone ride until the wheels fall off, and when they fall off I'll still be that nigga on the passenger side waiting on the tow truck." Mun joked.

"Yeah, I know, but I wouldn't ask you to do no shit like that. I know yo' steelo."

"Aye, y'all ready? Momma just called looking for Donk!" Quaylo yelled as she came through the door, removing her Dior shades, looking like a million bucks.

"I got you, but when we get situated at mommas, I really got some for you." Mun said as he handed the cashier a twenty-dollar bill.

"Ha, ha, ha. Let's go see what the lick read." Donk replied as he followed Mun out of the store. Donk's mind frame hadn't changed much and that's what everyone feared the most.

At a young age, Donk had always had sticky fingers, but as he grew he became more open and negligent to who saw him. If you tried to stop him in the process or intervene in any type of way, he would hurt you. You'd think after six years flat it would make you want to take a different route, but it only made Donk more of a menace.

As they cruised down Grove Street Donk hung out the window listening to the Lil Boosie throwback "Touchdown to Cause Hell". Quaylo hadn't stopped smiling since Donk walked out of the store.

For some reason Donk wasn't feeling Rico at all, but he remained cool. Donk turned around in his seat and eyed Quaylo curiously. "Lil niggga, what you been up to?" Donk asked.

"Chilling, getting to the money, trying to stay out the way." Quaylo was beautiful despite her dominant swag. She had her dreads into a tight bun to show off her smooth dark skin.

Donk kept interrogating her because he felt it was some things she was keeping to herself. Donk had been her protector since they were kids. When he would keep screw drivers and knives under his pillow so they're drunk stepfather wouldn't try nothing stupid. He was always overprotective of his big sister and Quaylo knew that, and that's why she could never bring herself to tell him how her and Rico had gotten so close. Shit, if Mun knew what transpired he would spazz out.

It all happened four years ago:

Rico and Mun went to Quaylo's spot to watch the Floyd Mayweather fight. It was a Saturday night. Mun had the Kush and Rico had the liquor. Quaylo had just moved into an apartment complex on the Southside so this was they're way of celebrating.

"Damn, sis, your new place the truth. It looked like you went to IKEA or somethin'!" Mun playfully shouted over the loud music.

Rico began laughing hysterically.

"Yeah, y'all keep laughing I'm gone have to kick y'all out of my shit once I really deck it out." Quaylo shot back.

Mun sat down and grabbed a magazine while placing his feet on the coffee table. Rico strolled into the kitchen to retrieve the cups and ice. Quaylo threw Mun the cigarillos and followed Rico into the kitchen.

"The Styrofoam cups in the pantry," Quaylo informed Rico while she grabbed a pineapple Fanta out the fridge. She loved

13

pineapple Fanta with peach Ciroc, even though she really wasn't much of a drinker.

Rico began to walk out of the kitchen when he looked back and saw Quaylo bent over, getting a bag of chips off the bottom shelf. That's when he crept up behind her and pressed his erection against her ass.

"Nigga, what the fuck you got going?" Quaylo asked as she spun around with a mug on her face.

"Damn, Quay, let a nigga hit. You be walking around here with those skimpy ass clothes on, teasing a nigga." Rico whispered in her ear as he roughly backed her into the wall, cupping her chin in his hand.

"Nigga, it ain't shit skimpy about my clothes; you just trippin'," Qualyo shot back, resisting his touch. Quaylo actually thought Rico was handsome but she wasn't sexually attracted to him. He was more like a brother to her. She'd known Rico for a few years now and she never looked at him in that type of way. It felt so awkward and weird that he was pushing up on her like that. "Nigga, I look at you like a brother. This shit isn't for us." Quaylo spoke through clenched teeth with a hint of uneasiness in her eyes.

Rico seemed unfazed by her response. He continued to use his hand to explore her body. Caught up in his own trance he began to forcefully slide his hand down her pants. Quaylo tried to remove his hand but he was too strong. She continued to struggle as she attempted to break free.

"Quit trying to fight this shit, girl." Rico mumbled as he easily shoved her hand out the way, using his other hand to play with her kitty. He then used his two fingers to pry her lips apart as he began to play with her clit.

Quaylo was still squirming to get away but Rico already noticed her biting her lip and her eyes roll to the back of her head. She slowly began to surrender to his touch.

"You like that?" Rico asked Quaylo while he gazed into her eyes.

She smiled and melted like butter on a hot stove. The vacancy in Rico's eyes made her crave him even more. Quaylo would never admit it, but his fingers felt good and her pussy was so wet. The way Rico was staring at her with those sexy, hazel eyes as he licked his pink, succulent lips only made her want to fuck him right then and there. She could feel and smell his breath as he deeply inhaled and exhaled.

"Aaaye, where the drinks at?" Mun yells from the living room, startling them.

Despite being appalled, Rico slowly removed his hands, stuck both his fingers inside his mouth, and smacked his lips while staring intensely at Quaylo. "Look, I know I came on strong, but I've been wanting to taste and feel you for so long. We gone go back in here and have a good time. I'm gone call you later on tonight and hopefully we can finish what we started," Rico stated before walking out and leaving Quaylo standing in the middle of the kitchen looking dumbfounded but appeased.

Quaylo still couldn't believe what had just occurred, but she did know one thing. She wanted more of Rico. Quaylo walked into the living room with a two-liter pineapple Fanta, and a bottle of peach Ciroc with a bag of sour cream and onion chips to hold them until the Rotel finished cooking.

"Damn. 'Bout time." Mun uttered while opening the bag of chips.

"Rico dumb ass dropped the ice so I made the nigga help me clean it up," Quaylo shot back.

Rico laughed to himself then sparked up the blunt while putting the TV on the fight.

"Aawww shit! The fight on!" Quaylo yelled, flopping down on the love seat.

Throughout the fight, Rico and Quaylo constantly exchanged glances. Neither one of them could wait for the fight to be over. Quaylo was so caught up she forgot about the Rotel.

"Oh shit!" Quaylo yelled, jumping to her feet and running to the kitchen. She turned off the stove and began to make the plates.

"One of y'all got to clean the dishes since I cooked," Quaylo joked while walking into the living room with their plates in each hand.

15

"Aight," Rico replied nonchalantly.

"K.O.! K.O.! Yeeeaaahhhh, run me my money!" Mun shouted with a mouth full of nachos as he jumped to his feet before reaching down to pick up his cell phone. While Mun was busy talking to someone on the other end of his phone, Rico winked at Quaylo.

"How much you bet, bro?" Quaylo ask.

"Five grand," Mun replied, sucking the cheese off his fingers.

"Can I have two?" Quaylo joked.

"That's cool," he replied, grabbing his car keys off the table. "I love you, sis. I had a good time, but me and Rico got some business to handle. I'm gon' call you tomorrow." Mun states as he headed toward the door.

Quaylo uncrossed her legs and hopped off the couch. "Nigga, y'all always busy, but since you leaving, can I get my two grand right now?" Quaylo asked as she followed them to the door.

"Girl, that's all you care about." Mun chuckled, digging into his pocket and peeling off twenty-five hundred dollars.

"Alright, Quay, see you tomorrow. Use that loot to pimp yo' shit out." Rico snickered as he walked out.

Nigga, if I give you this pussy you gon' be the one to deck my shit out. Quaylo thought. "Nigga, you funny." Quaylo laughed sarcastically before slamming the door.

QUAYLO

I turned up the volume on my Jeezy CD and began to clean up the house. Dirty cups and plates covered the small coffee table. I was bobbing my head to the beat when I noticed the screen on my phone light up.

I sprinted across the room to pick up my phone. It was a message from Rico.

Rico: Give me a hour I'm on my way.

Me: Okay

16

I sat the phone down, grinning from ear to ear. I ran through the house like a teenager getting ready for my first date. I never thought Rico could make me feel some type of way.

I scrubbed my body with Dove soap as the hot water descended down my back. I washed up real good and hopped out with nothing on but a towel. I sat on the edge of my bed and lubricated my skin with Palmer's Cocoa Butter Lotion and sprayed on my favorite Viva la Juicy fragrance. I walked inside of my closet and grabbed a lingerie piece out of a shopping bag that I purchased a couple of weeks with a Victoria Secret gift card Mun gave me. I slid into the pink and black bombshell bra and black lace boy shorts. I had a body females dreamed about even though I don't show it often. I mean, I didn't have a big, ghetto booty, but it was nice and plump; perfect for my shape; and my slim waist only enhanced the size of my Apple Bottoms. My perky C-cup breast were my most prized possession. I applied a coat of pink lip gloss and dimmed the lights before heading to the kitchen.

I was rummaging through the fridge when I heard a knock at the door. Before I could open the door all the way, Rico was all over me— grabbing me by my waist and forcefully shoving his tongue down my throat— but I was enjoying every minute of it. We tripped and stumbled on our way to the couch.

"Get naked," he demanded with pervious eyes.

I slowly removed my bra, revealing my bare breast and flickering my tongue across the nipple. This really put him on edge. He slowly whipped out his 9-inch dick and started stroking himself slowly as he watched me play with my tiddies. His dick was massive and elegant. The sight of it made my mouth water.

I couldn't take it anymore; I wanted to feel him inside of me now. I grabbed hold of his boxers and denim jeans, pulled them off and threw them on the floor.

"Bend over," he mumbled.

Without hesitating I spread my legs and bent over, using the arm on the couch to position my hands. He slipped on a condom and entered me slowly, one inch at a time. I reached back and used one of my hands to spread my butt cheeks so he could easily push the rest of himself inside of me. After a couple of deep and slow strokes I began to get used to the size.

"Damm, Quay, yo shit tight and wet."

I was throwing it back like a pro. "Oooohhhh, shit! Fuck me, Rico! Fuck me, daddy!" I yelled. It had been so long since I had something rock hard penetrating my insides. I had been sucking pussy for so long I forgot how good dick felt.

Rico used his hands to spread both my butt cheeks apart and began to pick up his pace. I slightly arched my back as the deep digging began.

"Oh my gawd, you—" I was so weak I couldn't even finish my sentence. "I'm 'bout to buss." I spoke through clenched teeth.

Suddenly he pulled out. I turned my head to see why he stopped, but he pushed my head down and entered me again. This time it felt like he was inside of me raw, no condom. Moans escaped from my mouth as he thrust himself deeper and deeper inside of me. I couldn't hold it any more. My legs began to shake uncontrollably as I exploded all over his monster. My kitty was throbbing with pain and pleasure. He grabbed a handful of my hair and gave me one last thrust as he released his seed into the condom. He slowly pulled out and passed out on the couch.

I wrapped my hair into a messy bun and sat across the room on the love seat. I couldn't take my eyes of him. I sat admiring his rippled upper body as his chest slowly heaved. I'm tripping already, I thought.

In the midst of my thoughts, Rico got up and walked toward me, where he hovered over me with his mans directly in my face.

"What you thinking about? Daddy dick?" He teased.

"Boy, I ain't worried about you, and now that you got what you wanted, what time you leaving?" I replied, refusing to feed into his bullshit.

Rico smirked and walked off, picking up his clothes off the floor before getting dressed. He grabbed his keys off the table and headed toward the bathroom. A few minutes passed and he walked past me nonchalantly before opening the door.

"Lock the door. I'll catch you later." He mumbled arrogantly.

"Alright," I shot back as I watched him walk out of the door.

I finally got up to lock the door and my knees felt weak, yet I felt so good; like a high, and Rico was the drug.

I stepped inside my kitchen and grabbed an ice cream out the fridge, then sat on the couch and logged into Facebook. I updated my status and continued to scroll down the page. A couple minutes later, after I got tired of being nosey, I decided to take a shower. When I entered the bathroom, I noticed the money and sheet of paper on the counter.

"I know you don't want for anything, but I just wanted to show you how much I appreciated that pussy. I hope to see you soon. Love, RICO."

Rico's little note had me smiling from ear to ear. I threw the note inside the trash bin and hopped in the shower. The whole time I reminisced on me and Rico's sex session. I couldn't believe how he put it down. I hated to admit it, but I think I'm hooked and I really don't give a damn. I just want it.

Now, here it is four years later and I'm still fucking this nigga.

CHAPTER 2
DONK
The Present

Me, Quaylo, Rico and Mun pulled up to my mother, Rochelle's house. Rochelle was 5'4", 135-pounds with a smile that will light up a room. Her hair was long and pretty. She had a dark complexion with a little petite frame, with lips like Angelina Jolie. She was a naturally pretty, and possessed the most peaceful aura. She was very simple— all she liked to do was listen to her blues music and get lit. We weren't as fortunate as the other kids growing up, but she did the best she could with her being a single parent. She didn't have a lot of different men around or used any hard drugs; she just struggled financially, and that reason alone made us take our own route. She hated the life we chose, especially me, but we were grown and on our own.

As soon as I hopped out the car, Rochelle ran up to me and wrapped her arms around my waist. I instantly inhaled her Dior perfume. "Hey, baby. I missed you so much. I'm so, so, so glad you're home." She spoke, choking on her tears.

I squeezed her tightly. I missed her so much. "I know, mama. I'm home for good. Quit crying. Let's go inside and celebrate."

We walked hand in hand into the house. Mun, Quaylo and Rico were already waiting inside.

"Man, bro, you better come eat what mama cooked!" Mun yelled.

"Dang, mama. I wish I would've known before I ate that cheeseburger." I joked as I flopped down on the couch.

Quaylo came from the kitchen with a plate for me.

"Damn, lil' sis. You still know a nigga, 'cause you already know I was just bullshitting."

I'm sitting on the couch chilling, enjoying my food when Quaylo runs out of the house to answer her phone. I happen to look back and Rico is eyeing her closely with a twinge of discomfort in his eyes. *It's some funny shit going on with them, and I'm going to find out*, I thought.

"So, baby, you gone stay here until you get on your feet?" Rochelle asked as she sat next to me with tears still in her eyes. Honestly, I planned to crash at Mun's place, but with her staring at me like this, it's no way I could tell her no. Besides, I missed my mom, and the same shit I could do at Mun's place I could do here.

"I'ma stay here for a few weeks, ma," I assured her as I wiped the tears from her face.

"Are you going to stay out of trouble this time, Dontrell?" I hated when she called me by first name.

"Yes, mama, I promise."

"Okay. I'm going to take your word for it, 'cause baby, I need you." She stated, looking into the depths of my soul. Rochelle always tried to keep a close eye on me.

At a young age I was in and out of juvie, only to return home telling her the same promise. All she ever wanted was for a nigga to change in some type of way, and I know by that she meant my hustle.

"Okay, well, I'm about to go holla at some breezies and I'll be back later, mama. Cool?" I joked with my fist out.

"Cool," she replied as she pounded fists with me.

I walked out the house looking for Quaylo and spotted her standing by the side of the driveway. "Awe! Yo' little ass done got grown. What you been up to?" I asked slowly walking toward her.

"Grown? Nigga, I'm older than you!" She joked.

"Where the hoes at?" Since we were younger, Quaylo always had a thing for women.

"That was one of my lil' thots I just got off the phone with. I can put you down with the sister if you want."

"Iight, do that, but let me ask you something. Who is ol' boy to you?" I questioned.

"Who? Rico?"

"Yeah, Rico." I replied, sounding sarcastic.

"Donk, damn! Nothing! He like another brother to me. He been around forever."

22

"Oh, yeah?" I smirked, yet starting into her eyes intensely. See, Quaylo must've forgot I've always been able to tell when she was lying.

"Yes, nigga; you crazy!" She shouted walking back toward the house.

"Yeah, whatever. Is you chilling with me and Mun? If so, we about to go."

"Hell yeah, I'm going, but I'll catch up with y'all later. Just hit me up!"

We pulled into the driveway of Mun's duplex home. It was a house I was unfamiliar with.

"Come on, nigga, this my lil' duck off." Mun said getting out of the car.

The neighborhood was unusually quiet and despite the size of the duplex you could tell this was an area for middle class and high-class residents.

"Damn, bruh, this bitch nice." I said looking around the house.

"Yeah, don't nobody know about this spot but you and Quay." Mun said smiling as he walked toward the back. Despite the feminine touch, the house was nicely furnished. A huge glass window decorated the dining room which gave a superior view to the outdoors. "I told you I had something for you." Mun said returning with a shoebox in his hand.

I removed the lid and inside was four stacks of hundred-dollar bills with a 9-millimeter chrome Beretta underneath the cash.

"Its five grand in each stack," Mun said rolling a blunt.

I stuck my fist out and dapped him up. I knew the nigga was getting it in, but I didn't know life was this good.

"Bro, I appreciate you for coming through for a nigga. Now, I can cop me a whip, some fits and whatever else I need until I shake back."

"Don't worry about your whip. Go open the garage."

I walked to the door that led to the garage and opened it. A smile quickly spread across my face as I slid my hand across the hood of the 2014 Cadillac CTS. It was black on black just how I liked it.

23

Mun tossed me the keys. "The registration and insurance is in your name, and all that is in my closet. Go get you one while I finish rolling this weed so we can bounce," he suggested anxiously.

I headed down the hallway to Mun's room. Pictures of Tupac hung along the walls. Pac had been his favorite rapper since he came out the womb. I entered Mun's room. It was pretty empty with just a flat screen and a king size bed. You could tell he didn't stay here often. I opened the door that was linked to the walk-in closet. It was boxes of shoes piled up to the ceiling and brand-new clothes hung from both racks. Mun's swag was official. Red Tru Religion v-neck shirt with all-white, trimmed in red Tru Religion shorts, and a pair of all white Air Forces.

"Awww, nigga, I forgot I had that bitch. I see you still got it," Mun said once I headed back to the living room.

"Hell yeah. I'm ready to bounce now!"

"Iight. I'm going to leave my car here and we gone get in you shit," Mun suggested, tucking the blunt behind his ear before dusting the residue off his jeans.

CHAPTER 3
MUNS

Me and Donk pulled up to the barbershop in South Dallas on South Boulevard. It was real roughish in the south. I knew Donk was about to get his Boosie fade. Nigga been having the same cut since middle school. I'm just elated that I stayed on top of my shit and was prepared for his return. We hopped out the car and went inside. As usual Big Mike had someone in his chair. I'm surprised he didn't have a line of niggas. Mike had been cutting hair for years. Since we were young we came to this very same shop.

"Awwww shit, my nigga! I missed you, boy!" Big Mike yelled as he approached Donk with open arms.

"Wassup, boy? I see you still on ya shit." Donk shot back.

"Who you got next?" I interjected.

"Oh, my nigga getting VIP service since it's his first day home." Big Mike replied.

My phone began to ring. "Hello?"

"Where you at?"

"Wassup?"

"It's 'bout that time."

"Damn, nigga, you on yo shit. Give me an hour I'm 'bout to be pulling up on ya." I ended the call with Rico diverting my attention back to Donk. Rico had run through his pack and was ready to re-up. "Man, Rico been moving them bricks quick as shit lately," I mumbled to Donk after Big Mike walked off.

"Oh yeah? That's wassup," Donk replied, rubbing his chin.

Matter of fact, since I'm down the street and Donk still waiting, I'll slide through right now, I thought. "Aye, lil' bro, I'm 'bout to ride around the corner real quick. I'll be right back." I assured Donk as I stood to my feet.

"Iigt," Donk replied as he handed me the car keys.

***

Lil' Tim was standing in the front yard serving a dope fiend when I pulled up. Lil' Tim was 14 years old. He had been working for me for about two years now. He wasn't no killer, but he could sell water to a fish. I liked the hustle in him. I usually don't condone in taking them in young, but I felt pity for the young soldier. What really just did it was when he approached me one day and told me he wanted to be just like me when he grew up. Since then I took him under my wing, and we been rockin' like a cut-off stockin'.

"What's up, Mun?" Lil' Tim yelled.

"What's good? Where Rico?"

"He in there." He replied pointing toward the door.

I walked in the crib and saw Rico on the money machine. When he noticed me, he seemed a bit shocked by my presence.

"Damn, nigga, you good?" I asked him quizzically.

"Yeah. Why you say that, boy?" He asked.

"I'm just saying, nigga, your pupils big as shit and you look a little shook up."

"Yeah, them boys been riding back and forth all day." He shot back.

"Oh yeah? Well I'm gon' have them birds later. I already hit him up."

"Okay, so what time you want me to be ready?"

"Oh, you good this time. Donk gon' ride with me so I can show him the ropes."

"Alright, cool," he replied nonchalantly.

"Where the bread? I left Donk at the barbershop. I got to go back and pick him up."

"Here's sixty-five. Let me go get the rest," Rico said as he went to the back room.

While I waited in the front for Rico to return, I start looking around curiously; something wasn't right. I didn't notice anything out of the ordinary, so I began to mellow down a bit. I moved the pillow to the side to sit on the sofa, and just when I was about to sit down, I saw a mirror covered with cocaine residue with a key sitting on top of it. *What the fuck? This nigga getting high?* A hundred thoughts began running through my mind while I focused in on what I just revealed. I shook my head in disbelief as I contemplated my next move. Damn, Rico, I thought.

Rule number one— do not get high on the supply. As pissed as I was, I still had a little sympathy toward Rico. I haven't tried coke, but I do know the shit can take you, fast. All I know is…if anything come up short, he'll just be hard to get where I'm at and I'd be damned if I let another nigga be my downfall. Fuck that. I gave him the game when I first introduced him to the shit. Besides, I ain't ever been in the business of babysitting.

Ah'Million

CHAPTER 4
RICO

Man, I did not expect this nigga Mun to show up so early. I shouldn't have ever hit that bump. Shit been getting out of hand and this shit was starting to take a toll on me. I done start dipping into my stash I tucked away for rainy days. Hustling forever is not part of the plan.

I walked back to the front room and gave Mun the rest of the money. He stared at me for a moment. I quickly looked away, avoiding eye contact.

"Iight, nigga, I'm about to head back to the barbershop to pick up Donk." Mun said walking toward the front door with the Lacoste shopping bag in his hand.

"Iight, fam. Stop by later to drop off that pack so I can keep shit in motion." I replied.

As soon as Mun reached for the door he paused and looked back. "Keep ya' head up and ya' nose clean." He suggested before walking out.

I knew exactly what he meant and I knew if I continued to let this drug do me, shit was eventually going to fall apart, but going broke is out of the question; and before I go broke I'll die trying to stay rich. I just got too much hustle in me for the bullshit. I just got caught up and it's hard to shake this shit.

I picked up my phone and called Quaylo. It rang twice then went to voicemail. She had to be ignoring my calls. She was probably with that dyke ass bitch. She gave me the pussy every blue moon. I don't know what it is but that pussy stayed on my mind. I know she playing hard to get 'cause I know my dick A-1 like steak sauce. I've been told too many times.

The real problem is she hasn't been feeling a nigga since she got that abortion. She felt like I pulled some slick shit, but in all reality, I just wanted to feel the pussy raw and uncut. I dialed Quaylo's number a few more times, but I continued to get the white lady. I began debating whether or not to call Donk. I heard through the streets the nigga get to the paper and I needed to make some extra moves real quick.

CHAPTER 5
QUAYLO

I saw Rico's name pop up on my screen, but I wasn't feeling him at the moment. So, I ignored his call yet again. I was at my young bitch, Nina's house. She picked me up last night and I dropped her off at a room with some dude she met at the club and circled the block a few times before I doubled back and entered the room, taking the nigga for everything he had. I gave her a quarter of the five g's and kept the rest. She really didn't care if I paid her or not, she just enjoyed being in my presence. Me and Nina were sitting on the couch watching Love and Hip Hop. She used her fingers to comb through my hair while my head rested on her breast. Nina was beautiful. She was Puerto Rican and black with long, jet black, curly hair. She had big green bedroom eyes and her lips resembled the actress Megan Good. We had been kicking it for a month, and even though I was low key addicted to Rico's dick, I was really digging Nina. I loved the way she treated me and catered to my every need.

"Bae, what time you leaving to go spend time with your brother?" She asked me.

"In about an hour or so."

"What's his name again?"

"Donk."

"Oh yeah. I forgot." Nina responded twirling her hair around her fingers. "Quay, I got a lick." She leaned up.

"Wassup? Rap?"

"This nigga that came to the club last night was splurging left to right, ordering buckets of ones, expensive bottles, and when he called me over to his section, he had so much dope. I know it was more where that came from," Nina said as she began to search my eyes, biting down on her lip.

"Alright. Get to it, and when you get everything set up, hit me up."

"Okay, baby." Nina responded with a kiss.

I grabbed a fist full of her hair and slid my tongue in her mouth while I kissed her slow and passionately. As moans escaped from her mouth, I slid my hand inside her green, lace boy shorts. Her pussy was soaked and I hadn't even touched her. Sex with Nina was amazing. She was about her paperwork and she was a down ass bitch. I reached further down to massage her clit when my phone lit up. This time it was Donk.

I slid my hand out of her panties and sucked her juices off my fingers before answering my phone. "Hello?" I spoke anxiously into the phone.

"What's up, lil' sis?"

"Chilling. You ready to link up?"

"Hell yeah. I'll be there in ten minutes."

"Bet," I responded as I hung up the phone and began to get dressed. I grabbed a pink and navy blue Polo shirt, white and navy-blue Polo shorts with a pair of navy blue and dark brown Ralph Lauren loafers. I really wasn't too fond of heels and dresses; only occasionally. "Aaye! I'm gone come through later on. Alright?" I assured Nina while folding my collar and adjusting my yellow gold rope necklace that hung to the middle of my breast.

"I know, bae. You always do. I know how close you are with your brothers. It's his first day out. Turn up. I'm happy for you."

"That's why I fuck with you." I chuckled, cupping her chin as I pecked her on the lips.

CHAPTER 6
DONK

Me and Mun headed back to Rochelle's house to meet up with Quaylo. It's been a minute since I've seen some bitches bust it open, so tonight we were hitting up Club DG's. I heard the bitches were bad and classy, and I was more than ready. Being locked away all those days had me feeling some type of away.

I pulled up to Rochelle's house. She was sitting on the porch with Rhonda. Rhonda had always been around, and even when we were growing up they've been the best of friends. I spotted the bodice and blunt in her hand as soon as I jumped out the car. I could hear her talking shit. This lady loved to regulate for nothing.

"Hey, baby," Rochelle yelled like she just didn't see a nigga a few minutes ago. This lady was childish. She sat, waving her arms in the air and snapping her fingers to the music. My grandmother raised her on the blues and she'd been loving it ever since.

"Rochelle? Girl, is that Donk? Girl, he done got big and handsome! Donk how old are you now?" Rhonda asked.

Before I could get the words out my mouth, Rochelle cut in. "Rhonda, don't play with me, with your old ass. You won't get a chance to take him. He don't need no damn cougar!"

Rhonda began laughing hysterically while trying to defend her remark. I jogged to the front of the yard once I spotted Quaylo pull up to the side of the curb in her pink Dodge Challenger. She opened the door and Young Jeezy blasted from the speakers. She stepped out sporting a nice Polo outfit, looking like new money. Her 14-karat gold rope chain and white gold 24-karat tennis bracelet glistened tremendously. *She was beautiful*, I thought. When it came to Quaylo, she was my weakness. She was my everything. She even did my bid with me. I never went without letters, commissary, pictures or nothing. It's two things I cherish in this world and it's love and loyalty, and she showed me exactly that. Don't get me wrong, Rochelle and Mun were there, too every step of the way, especially financially, but Quay helped me a lot mentally.

Growing up, mama had a psycho boyfriend and I always felt one day he'll tweak and try and do something to one of us. I slept in Quay's room every night with different weapons under my pillow. One day, he even put uncooked white rice on the kitchen floor and made me and Mun kneel on top of it. Rochelle didn't know about the rice incident, but she knew about the beatings. She used to say little to nothing, maybe because we only got beat every once in a while. I used to hate that motherfucker, but he knew I meant business by the way I looked at him.

"Hey, brother! Nigga, I'm ready to show you what you been missing!" Quaylo yelled as she playfully slapped me on my arm with her car keys.

I just smiled real big and said, "Alright, we ready! Mun?" I yelled as I walked over to the passenger's door of Quaylo's car.

Mun came jogging toward us. He rocked a low fade, and was dressed in a lime green and white AKOO fit with all-white low top Air Forces. "Look, y'all, I'm gone hop in my shit 'cause I got to handle some business after the club, and ain't no telling which one of y'all hoes ain't coming home tonight." He chuckled.

"Iight, lead the way. I'm ridin with Quay," I replied as I climbed into the passenger seat. Young Jeezy's *Way Too Gone* blasted through the speakers as Quaylo put the pedal to the metal.

I gazed out the window scoping out the different views of the new stores and buildings that were now open. The shit still felt like a dream. Just a few hours ago I was riding my bunk, listening to a bullshit ass country station 'cause some dumbass was fucking with the satellite and knocked off all the stations.

I glanced down at my phone when I noticed the screen light up. *How the fuck he get my number?* I scowled as I read the text.

Rico: Aye, whenever you not busy I need to holla at you about some business. This Rico.

What the fuck? I thought. I quickly diverted my attention out the window. I didn't have a clue what Rico could possibly want, but I know it can wait 'til later.

I was so intrigued by the foreign cars in the parking lot of the club. Rolls-Royce, Ferraris. Porches, and Bentleys were parked throughout the lot. All the big money was out tonight. Quaylo and Mun had all the connects. Mun knew the bouncer at the door who let us take our burners in.

"Mun, I know you doing big thangs, fam, but please don't kill nobody," the bouncer said grinning as he gave Mun a firm handshake.

The club was huge inside. There were four different stages with different exotic-looking, butt-naked women on each of them. You had one female doing pole tricks and the other shaking her ass. I could smell the money in the air, but my intentions were to chill and have a good time. It had been a minute since I was in the presence of a woman, and I just wanted to have a good time. We headed to the VIP section where we were greeted by a sexy ass waitress.

She looked as if she were black and Asian. She had tight eyes, high cheek bones and some sexy, juicy lips, with long, jet-black hair which was parted down the middle. When she spoke, her accent was so sexy, and it made my dick hard.

"Hey, Mun! Is there anything I can get you all today?" She asked while resting her hand on her hip.

"Today is my lil' brother's day, so whatever he wants is what we're drinking today, Persuasia." Mun replied looking at me for assurance.

"Don Perignon and Peach Ciroc for Quaylo."

"That's it? You are incredibly handsome, by the way. Mun never told me about you," she said.

"How long you been working here?"

"About two years."

"See, I just got from doing a six-year bid, but if you want, you can take your apron off and chill with me for the night."

"Damn, you fine! But I still got to live after tonight, boo. What about when I get off?" She suggested.

"Your loss. We'll see. Go get the drinks for now. I'm parched."

Persuasia smirked and then walked away to retrieve the drinks. She had ass for days and nice, big, perky breast to go with it. Her hair hung right on top of her ass as she sashayed to the bar.

"She everybody freak?" I asked Mun before easing into the chair comfortably.

"Nah. The bitch low-key and she never came my way. She a school girl, I think." Mun replied.

"And she don't fuck with females." Quaylo cut in with a big grin on her face.

I just cut my eye at her and commenced to looking around the club. I wasn't too fond of that gay shit, but then again it was better than hearing her ramble on about niggas.

Persuasions came and set the drinks on the table "How many ladies? And do you have a preference?" She asked.

"Nah, I don't discriminate. Bitches is bitches. You can send six," I responded.

I guess my last comment offended her 'cause I noticed her nostrils began to flare. "They'll be over shortly," Persuasia responded walking off.

I slapped her on the ass right before she passed me and she looked back and gave me a wink. A few minutes later, six thick strippers bent the corner heading our way. My dick had already start jumping and the bitch hadn't even bounced on my shit. Migos' *Pipe it Up* blasted through the club. The DJ was doing his thang. The light skinned girl in the front was tatted like a biker boy.

"I want you." I pointed while looking into her direction, instantly noticing something familiar about her. "What's yo name, ma?"

"Poca," she responded. The name didn't register to me, but I know I've seen those eyes before. I just couldn't place it. "You are so handsome. I never seen you in here before." Poca spoke while making her butt cheeks clap. She did it with ease.

"I know. I just came home." I replied as I grabbed my bucket full of one's and slid a handful inside her thongs. The longer I sat, the uneasier I felt. The shit was really starting to bother me. I knew this chick from somewhere. I looked over at Mun and Quaylo who seemed to be enjoying themselves. Mun was getting a lap dance by a thick snow bunny. She had the nigga's head all between her legs. Quaylo must've came here quite often. She knew all the girls' names. As soon they hit the door, one of the strippers was doing the splits while Quaylo poured Ciroc down the crack of her ass.

Persuasia came back with more drinks. She sat the drinks on the table before sitting next to me. "Oh, so you like to see thick bitches shake they ass?" She asked sarcastically, eyeing me intensely. She was so close I could feel the warmth of her breath on my cheek. If it didn't smell like Similac I probably would've spazzed out on her ass for disrespecting me.

I slightly chuckled at her jealousy. I thought it was kind of cute. "Look, ma, that's why I came to a *strip club*— to watch bitches shake they ass." I retorted.

"You right. I'm tripping. Enjoy yourself, sweetie. Here's my number. Make sure you use it." With that being said, she stood to her feet, slung her hair over her shoulder as she walked past Poca, slightly brushing her arm. She was already in her feelings and I hadn't even blew on the pussy. That's the shit I don't like.

Poca was really making a nigga feel good, but I still couldn't shake the fact that I knew this bitch. Not being able to hold it in anymore, I called, "Aye, ma." I tapped her on the shoulder.

She quickly stopped bouncing on my dick and turned around.

"Aye, where I know you from?"

"I don't know, daddy. I dance state to state, but to be honest I don't ever recall seeing you. I do want to get out of here so I can show you what I'm really about."

I eyed the bitch skeptically. The eyes never lie, and I don't give a damn about what she was saying. I know we've crossed paths before, but it could've been at a store, school, another club, anywhere. I'm just gon' drop it and enjoy myself for the first time in a long time. "Aight, ma. We can get a room once we leave the club." I glanced over at Quaylo who's looking at me over her champagne glass. I just chuckled to myself. That girl is so nosey.

Once we locked eyes she got up and sat next to me. "Bro, I'm glad you home. Now everything is back how it used to be. I'm also glad to see you enjoying yourself," Quaylo said as she wrapped her arm around my neck.

"Yeah, that liquor got you all sentimental and shit, but to be honest, I'm ready to go. I got some pussy waiting on me."

"Nigga, go! What you waiting on? We good. Me and Mun do this shit every weekend. Besides, you better get ol' girl while she hot, 'cause I don't see her too often. I think she a out-of-town chick."

"Yeah, I got to go pick this pack up anyways. I wanted you to roll with me, but I'm good. it's just another pick up." Mun cut in as he stood to his feet.

"You sure? If not, I'm rolling with you. You know it's always business first before anything else." I shot back.

"Nigga, we good!" Quaylo and Mun spoke in unison.

"Iight, shit. Then, I'll hit y'all up tomorrow."

CHAPTER 7
MUN

We all exited the club, going out separate ways. However, the night was still young. I called Lito, my connect, and made plans to link up. Lito was an older Italian dude. He had the best coke I ever came across and the nigga's money was taller than Kevin Durant. Me and Lito had been doing business for about two years now. I never really contacted him earlier. I had just told Rico that 'cause I didn't want him rolling with me, pissed off at what I found underneath the pillow on the sofa.

I've been nothing but good to this nigga and this is how he repay me? He can't even keep it real with me, but I realized a long time ago that favor ain't fair. If you lie, you'll cheat and steal, and I'm thinking against the idea of sitting around waiting on the inevitable.

Lito wanted to meet up at the AMC 30 movie theater. Shit was coming up missing and shipments were getting busted so he was doing all his big shit on his own. The drive to AMC 30 was about thirty minutes away from the club. As I neared the red light on Bexar Street, I reclined my seat and fired up a Kush blunt, as I inserted Yo Gotti's latest mix tape.

I was so glad Donk came home when he did. It was right on time. He's the only nigga I trust to take Rico's place.

Despite being in deep thought, I glanced back at the black Honda that had been following me since I pulled out of the club's lot. At first, I gave it the benefit of the doubt, but nigga been following me for a couple minutes now. I bust a left on Military Street just to see if I was tripping. My assumptions were correct. I wasn't tripping, I was really being followed.

I pulled out my phone and called Lito.

"What's up, Mun? I'm down the street," he said.

"Look, Lito, someone is following me, so change of plans. I'll call you tomorrow and we can link up then."

"Where are you? You good?"

"Yeah, I'm about to hit my people up; I'm good."

"Alright, be safe. You know I'm always on standby."

"Bet." I quickly hung up the phone with Lito and bust a U-Turn, heading back to my side of town. Instead of going to my spot, I took a detour toward the projects where my shooters were. I didn't want to call Donk, so I decided to call Rico.

I couldn't make out the driver's face due to the dark tint on the windows, but this shit wasn't a coincidence. It was some shit in the game. Straight up.

CHAPTER 8
QUAYLO

I laughed to myself as I puffed on the blunt behind the wheel of my Challenger. I had been following Donk since he left the club. I was the strip club queen, yet I didn't know hardly anything about the bitch. She rarely ever worked. I know Donk's capable of taking care of himself, but I don't give a damn. Better safe than sorry. I was just skeptical about the whole idea, because I didn't know this bitch's background. Besides, I didn't have shit better to do. I'm pretty sure Nina was asleep.

Damn, just like a nigga to take a bitch to a cheap motel. But she's the one driving, so no telling whose decision it was. Damn, Donk, the least you could've done was treat the bitch to the Hilton so she could've grabbed her some breakfast the next morning, I thought.

I know Donk didn't realize he was being trailed, 'cause this bitch had him thinking with his dick. As I sat in the parking lot of the Motel 6, I watched Poca stumble out of the driver's side. They must have been drinking in the car 'cause she didn't have not one drink in the VIP section. I had been watching her from the moment Donk chose her out of the group of women. Donk hopped out and grabbed her by the waist, guiding her toward the room.

Once they entered the room, a few minutes passed and reality quickly set in. I then realized I'll be out here for a minute, so I decided to call Nina.

"Hello?" She softly spoke into the phone.

"What you doing?"

"I was asleep. What time is it? When are you coming home?"

"I'm out and about right now. Give me about two hours and I'll be there, but don't wait up for me. Go ahead and go back to sleep."

"Alright. Goodnight, and be careful."

"Goodnight."

I puffed on my joint and logged into my Facebook as I reclined my seat all the way back. Different females stayed in my inbox, but I wasn't too fond of social media dating. Some chicks be using fake pictures and all that shit; I refuse to let a bitch catfish me.

An hour passed and I still sat in the same position. The volume on my radio was on low as I bobbed my head to Gucci Mane's new mixtape.

Man, I'm tripping. This nigga just getting some pussy. I'ma stake out for another hour then burn out, I thought. "Damn, this raggedy ass motel got security?" I asked myself, squinting to improve my view, but as the car got closer, I realized it was an all black Crown Victoria, not a patrol car. The windows weren't tinted so I could see perfectly inside the car. The pipes were loud and despite the cracked windshield, the car looked practically new.

Two black dudes occupied the car— one with dreads and the other one rocked a low fade. The one in the driver's seat was on the phone with someone. I could see him looking around the motel, but I couldn't help but notice his facial expression change once he looked in the direction of Donk's room.

Unfortunately, he parked right beside me, but I stopped stressing on the fact of being seen. My tint was so dark that the police fucked with me about it numerous times. I didn't want to make any assumptions, however I never been a naïve bitch. I baffled with the idea of calling Donk, but then realized I can't go wrong with alerting him; just in case.

I grabbed my phone and called Donk. I became frustrated after hearing his phone ring and ring until it went to voicemail. After numerous attempts, I began to panic. *How the hell am I going to forewarn this motherfucka if he won't answer his phone*, I thought.

The dudes still hadn't made a move, giving me more time to contemplate on my next move. I reached inside my secret compartment underneath my steering wheel and grabbed my 9-millimeter and attached my silencer, before reaching inside my MK bag and clutching my 38-revolver, sticking it inside my sock. Time passed but still no call from Donk. I didn't want to call Mun on a dry ass mission. These niggas probably not even here for him.

The Kush got me paranoid but I'm gone be strapped and ready just in case. My gut instincts were telling me I wasn't tripping and these grimy ass niggas were here for my brother, and since I was young my gut never lead me wrong. My palms were sweating and all I could think was, *He already lost his life to the system time and time again, but I'd be damned if I lose him forever. If they think this gone be an easy job, they got another thing coming.* I looked to the left inside the Crown Vic and seen the nigga checking the clips inside the burners. I squinted to try and decipher the model of the guns, however I still couldn't tell. *It's about to get real, but at least I'm not a sitting duck.* Immediately I'm snapped out of my thoughts when I hear the engine cut off. *Shit! Think, Quay. Fuck it, it's just another body.*

The dude in the driver's seat seemed a bit agitated, but he still hopped out and tucked his ratchet into his jeans, then signaled for the other dude to get out. By the way they were dressed, you could tell the niggas wasn't no average stick-up kids. You could tell they were getting paid. They slowly eased the doors closed and slowly began to cross the parking lot. There was no light in the lot whatsoever. You could tell the bulb in the light post was old as fuck and hadn't been changed. There were a few parked cars scattered throughout the lot.

I slowly opened my car door and crouched beside my car. I was nervous as hell, but I'd be damned if I allowed something to happen to my little brother. I eased the door closed before lifting up on to my tip-toes and darting across the lot. I quickly crouched behind a gray Toyota Camry. The cool breeze caused my teeth to chatter as I slowly made my way around to the side of the car. I was right behind them, however they were still a few feet away from the door. "Fuck this shit," I said to myself as I slowly raised up and cautiously walked behind the niggas with my burner in hand.

My suspicion came out to be exactly what I expected. The mothefukas were here for Donk.

Ring! Ring! Ring! Ring!

My cell phone rang as I quickly fidgeted with the device to deactivate the volume. "Shit!" Before I could power off my phone, two burners were pointed at my head. I tightly gripped the handle on my strap, angry at myself for allowing these niggas to put me in such a risky position. I just knew I was a dead bitch, but at least the shots would alert Donk. I lowered my head and prepared for the inevitable as I whispered a silent prayer.

Boom! Boom! Boom! Boom!

I quickly touched my chest and my lower body to see if I had been hit, when I looked down and saw both the dudes sprawled out on the pavement with holes the size of baseballs in their faces. *What the fuck*, I thought, trying to see past the gun smoke.

Donk stepped over the two bodies that lay in front of me, grabbing me by the arm. "Come on. Let's go. The laws gone be all over this place in a minute." Donk whispered as he softly shoved me in my lower back, guiding me back to the car.

"The engine still running. You drive." I told Donk as I walked to the passenger's side and hopped in.

For a few seconds the car was silent. Neither of us had anything to say or know how to say it. Suddenly, Donk chuckles. He was weird like that. "You know, Quay, I didn't actually think you were following me, I just thought you wanted to take yo' bitch to the same telly." He quoted with a smile on his face, like he just didn't body two niggas.

"Well, shit, I didn't think you noticed, but I only followed you 'cause I know what type of nigga you is and I didn't know ol' girl. She usually act real stuck up and stand offish, and it was just crazy to me how she was so open and friendly with you." I replied, still slightly shook up. I'd never been so close to death.

"Well, I 'preciate ya' for looking out for a nigga, but you got to be on your toes. What if I didn't peep the play? You could've gotten killed, Quay," Donk stated, sounding concerned. "See, I peeped the bullshit when the bitch couldn't even suck my dick 'cause she was too busy running back and forth to her phone. One thing I know for sure is when a nigga with some money is in a bitch presence, don't nothing else matter but more money. So, I felt then it was some fuckery going on. I done got so many niggas set up I know all the moves, but what really topped it off is from the jump I noticed the familiarity in her eyes. I knew I had seen her before, but I couldn't place it. Well after I murked the bitch I picked up her phone and seen the picture of her and a nigga. A nigga named Josh I robbed and killed a couple years ago." Donk informed.

"Damn. That's deep. That shit happened over six years ago. Who is Josh?"

"Josh her baby daddy. You know me. Fuck a mask; I bare-face my shit, and after I laid everybody down, I finished checking the rooms and the bitch was hiding in the closet. She was pregnant at the time, but it didn't make me no difference. When I lifted my tool to off the bitch, I heard the police pull into the driveway. So, I threw my duffle bag over my shoulder and ran out the back. My intentions were to take care of that, but I end up getting locked up."

"Damn, nigga, I thought I was dead. Here I am trying to pro-tect you, and like always you end up protecting me." The police car sped past us, going in the opposite direction. I looked over at Donk and smiled as a sense of relief came over me. "Welcome home, bro. They don't make them like you no more."

"Yeah, a lot of niggas faking like they glad to see me home, but I know all the love fake."

A lot of dudes envied Donk, but you'll never know it.

"Fuck em," we both spoke in unison.

Ah'Million

CHAPTER 9
RICO

Damn, it's 1:00 a.m. and Mun still hadn't dropped those birds off. I'm glad I still got me a little something leftover or I'll be in this bitch shaking like a stripper. I texted Donk a couple of hours ago, but the nigga still hadn't responded. I guess I'll try again later. I browsed through my text messages and hit the resend button on the text I sent him earlier. If Mun haven't come by yet, he's not going to come. I'll just hit him up tomorrow. I hated the fact I was hiding things. Since day one he has always had my back. To be honest, he'll understand and help me out, but then again, I don't want to look weak.

I reached over and grabbed my phone off the table. I commenced to calling Nicki, a chick I met at the strip club a few days ago. Nicki was one of the baddest strippers I done seen at a club. As soon as I laid eyes on her I knew I had to have her.

"What's up, baby?" I stated in my LL voice.

"Hey, boo. What you getting into this late?" She replied.

"That's what I'm trying to figure out. Come out. Pull up on me."

"Okay. Text me the address." She chuckled.

"Bet."

Nicki put you in the mind of a thicker Christina Millian. I needed to get up in something tight and wet anyways to take my mind off everything else. I walked into the kitchen and went inside my stash. I grabbed my personal pack so me and shawty can turn up in this bitch.

I really didn't plan on spending any major quality time with shawty, just a quick wam, bam, thank you, ma'am. I took a look in the mirror before splashing my face with water, which didn't help; I still looked high as hell.

Knock! Knock! Knock!

I walked to the front of the house to see who was at the door, and there stood Nicki looking like a model. I stuck my pistol in my front pocket and answered the door. I gave shawty a hug, noticing her Honda parked in the driveway. "Damn, ma. I thought you were riding luxury."

She slapped me on the arm playfully and said, "Nigga, that's my duck off. I had shit to do."

"Oh, okay." I replied sarcastically. *Shit, as much pussy as she pop, she should be in a Range Rover*, I thought.

"Nigga, and so what if that's my car? Why you complaining? What you gon' do about it?"

"Not a damn thang! Stop talking and let's get to it." I said as I tossed the dope to her and grabbed a bottle of Hennessey out of the pantry. Soon as I walked back into the living room Nicki already had my shit lined up and was stripping out of her thin maxi dress.

I looked her up and down before placing the bottle of Hennessey on the table. I immediately grabbed the tray and snorted two lines, while she began to pour us shots into the empty glasses. Something about that Tony made a nigga feel like the man of the hour.

Ring! Ring! Ring!

My eyes grew to the size of golf balls when I looked down at my screen and saw Mun's name. "Hello?" I asked calmly, trying to sound as sober as possible.

"Aye, nigga, I'm on my way through. Someone followed me from the club so I had to switch up the plan."

"Someone did what?" I yelled, infuriated at the thought of Mun's life being in danger.

"I know, nigga, that's what I was thinking. Who the fuck done grew enough balls to try and get at me?"

"Hell nah! Fuck that! Pull up on me. You know where I'm at."

CHAPTER 10
DONK

Even though I made it out with me and my sister's life, I was still a bit perturbed. That bitch must have really wanted my head 'cause she got at me my first night out. Even if the bitch would've played it cool, I still would've had a plan B 'cause Quaylo had her big eye on me the whole time. "Aye, Quay. We not gon' say nothing to mama about this." I said as I looked over at her and she was fast asleep, mouth wide open, Glock in hand. I just laughed to myself. She always got that damn burner and still managed to get caught slippin' but it's cool, 'cause as long as I got air in my lungs I'm gon' be there to protect her every time.

I merged onto interstate I-30 and headed to Rochelle's house when my phone rang.

"Lil' bro?" Mun spoke calmly into the phone.

"What's up, fam? Where you at?" I asked concerned.

"Aye, meet me at the spot. Some shit came up and I need to holler at you, ASAP."

"You got it. I'm on my way."

I hit the next exit and headed south as I cruised the streets. I jammed to J. Cole. He rapped: *"There's no such thing as a life that is better than yours. No such thing, no such thing."* I wondered what was up with Mun. He sounded a bit annoyed. Everybody already know my reputation. Only a fool would fuck with my loved ones. I chewed the inside of my lip as I tightened my grip on the steering wheel.

"Damn, nigga, slow down," Quay said with sleep still in her eyes.

"Oh, you woke now?" I asked.

"How long was I sleep?"

"Not long. Look, we on our way to the spot. Mun said something came up."

Quaylo quickly sat up in her seat as her eyes widened. "Something like what?"

"I don't know, but we about to find out and it bet not have nothing to do with that nigga Rico." I stated. Since day one I never liked the nigga, especially once I peeped the funny shit between him and Quay. He didn't come off to me as a real nigga, he was more like a counterfeit in my eyes.

"Why Rico?" She asked, looking puzzled.

"I don't know. I just don't like the nigga."

"I figured you didn't, but you don't like hardly anybody, Donk."

I didn't respond, I just glanced at her as I threw the car in park and hopped out. Mun's Magnum was already parked in the driveway. Quaylo was right behind me as we walked through the door.

Mun was seated at the bar and Rico was standing at the small table inside the kitchen. Once they spotted me and Quaylo they both made their way into the living room.

"What's up, fam?" Mun asked as he dapped me up.

"What's up with you?" Quaylo interjected.

"How y'all end up together? I thought you was with ol' girl?" Mun said, looking confused.

"It's a long story. You tell me what's going on with you first." I said before sitting down on the sofa.

"I was followed when I was on my way to meet up with Lito. I don't know who it was. All I know is they were driving a black Honda Accord with light tint on the windows. They followed me from the club all the way to Military Street. When I realized I was being followed I took a couple of back streets to see if I was tripping, but they continued to follow me. When I turned around to go in the opposite direction, they continued to follow me. When I turned out, they drove right past me. I was a little shook, because I thought they were going to pull alongside me and start blasting."

"Fuck! I'm gon' kill me a nigga! Somethin' told me to go with you. Instead I chose to fuck with that slick ass bitch.

"I thought once Donk came home shit would get better, but niggas want y'all dead." Quaylo spoke as she eyed Mun and I closely.

50

"Aye, Mun, you know my loyalty runs deep. Y'all like family. I'm going to keep my eyes and ears to the streets. Everybody just need to tighten shit up around here." Rico said.

"My shit tight. I don't know 'bout yo' shit." I said sizing Rico up.

"Look out, Donk. You been throwing shade since you got home. I ain't trying to take yo spot. Yo fam looked out for me. I feel like I owe Mun my life."

"Aight," I replied, dismissing Rico. I didn't want to continue to converse with the nigga. Shit just got real, but see this shit ain't on me, it's *in* me and I'm built like that. I live for this type of shit, and I enjoy what I do. Mun sell dope, Quaylo do whatever she do, and I kill and take shit, but I guarantee you, a bitch will not be my downfall. Fucking with a bitch got me fucked on two different accords. I could've just rolled with Mun and none of this would've happened. Rico looked as if he was in deep thought, but I paid him no attention.

"Look, I just want us all to be more cautious. We all we got. We can't afford to take a loss." Mun said as he looked at me and Rico.

"You need me to take care of something?" Quaylo asked anxiously, always ready for a task.

"I just want you to find out who was following me. Shit, you know more people than I do, so just stay on your toes and put your ears to the streets." Mun said.

"Alright," Quaylo responded as she went into her pocket and retrieved her phone.

"Let me holler at you real quick, Mun." I said and walked toward the bar. "So, you know the lil' hoe from the club tried to set me up to get whacked by two niggas? I was able to pick up on it once we were in the room. So, I popped the bitch. Well, on the way out the door I seen two niggas standing in front of my room, so I went out the window, came around from the side and silenced they ass, but guess who was standing right there when the smoke cleared?"

"Who?" He asked astonished by everything he was hearing.

"Quaylo. I guess something happened and they spotted her 'cause the straps were pointed toward her when I came out blasting. Come to find out Quaylo followed me cause she was skeptical about the bitch."

"Damn, Quay ass always up to somethin'. Did you ever find out exactly who the bitch was?"

"You remember that nigga Josh that stayed in Mesquite? He cut hair and sold dope all out the same house? Well, I hit his ass a few months before I got locked up and murked him while she was in the closet hiding, and soon as I was about to kill her, I heard the laws pulling into the driveway, so I bounced and let her make it."

"Josh ol' pussy ass. That nigga wasn't no real dope boy. I remember that lame. He moved from the suburbs and thought he was a hood nigga. Damn, so is you good now?"

"Yeah, that's the only witness I ever let live to witness any motherfucking thang."

"Cool. Let me ask you something."

"Rap."

"What's yo beef with Rico?"

"I got my reasons."

"Well, between me and you, the nigga fucking with that Tony Montana."

"Word? So you gon' cut him off? Once a junkie, always a junkie, fam."

"Nah, not yet. I don't want to cut him off completely. With his line of work, he needs to be sober and focused, but you should be able to use him on your team."

"You really fuck with this cat, huh? Alright, I got you and I'll help run shit here if you need me, but look at this." I said, pointing at Rico and Quaylo who seemed to be having a heated discussion.

"That's why I don't like the nigga. I'm telling ya' it's some funny shit going on between them two."

CHAPTER 11
QUAY

This nigga was really on my motherfucking nerves, that's the reason I ignore his calls. I come over here to check on Mun and he gets all up in my face interrogating a bitch. He did look sexy going off, but damn, he needed to get out of his feelings. He always had some type of bullshit going on, but I never seen him like this.

"Okay. Okay. Okay, Rico, you got it, so what? What's the conclusion?" I said with my hands on my hip.

"I just want to be alright with you. Why you got to act like this? Like we don't be tearin' it up?" Rico stated with a smile on his face.

"See, you play too much. That's why I don't fuck with yo' red ass! Nigga, you ain't no damn Tyrese!"

"Okay, okay. On some real shit, I cut for you in ways I didn't think I could. I want you to leave them hoes alone and these streets and let a nigga do right by you, and take care of you."

"Boy, I'm not about to play with you." I replied turning my back.

Rico spun me around. "Man, I'm for real. I want us to tell Mun and Donk so we won't have to continue to creep around like we're kids. I want you to be my woman."

I couldn't believe what I was hearing. I wouldn't mind laying down and waking up to Rico's fine ass. "Okay, I'll think about it, but for now I'll start answering my phone and responding to your text." I said walking away, leaving his ass standing there. I walked into the kitchen where Mun and Donk sat, and to my surprise they both were staring at me, smirking. "What's up?" I asked, throwing my hands up.

"You tell us." Mun replied while Donk eyed me so intensely it felt as if he were looking right through me.

"Nothing. Hold on. Is this about Rico? He was just telling me about this lick. I think he want to start jacking."

"Oh yeah?" Donk asked, rubbing his chin.

"Yeah."

53

"Well, I'm going to holler at the nigga."

"Well, I'm gon' catch up with y'all later. I'm about to duck off and catch me some zzzz's." I told Donk and Mun as I hugged them both before retrieving my keys from the countertop. I walked toward the door and gave Rico a friendly hug. He just shook his head and kept contemplating. *I wonder what it is he's thinking about.*

The ride to Nina's house was pretty silent. I didn't even bother to turn the volume up on the radio. I was really thinking about Rico and everything he said to me earlier. I never been with a dude and I do love Rico. The dick is amazing, but it's hard to decipher his motives. What if he starts trying to control me and shit? I got a lot to think about. I grabbed my phone out of the cup holder and texted Nina to let her know I was on my way. So much shit in one day, but I'll do it all again. It's life. Especially the life I live. One day I want to wake up living normal life. There're only two things that come from the street life and that's jail or death. Sometimes I regret ever fucking Rico. Because of him I did something I'll forever be sorry for.

I pulled into the parking spot in front of Nina's building. I was exhausted. I put my phone on silent and stepped out of the car. I looked around cautiously before unlocking the door to her crib. "Nina?" I yelled, dropping my keys on the counter.

"Yes, baby? I'm in the shower." She responded.

I walked into the bathroom. "Where you been?" I asked curiously.

"I was chilling with the nigga I told you about."

"So, what's up?"

"Give me another day or two and I'll be able to put somethin' into motion."

Nina looked so sexy but I was so exhausted I didn't have the strength to fuck her. I walked into the bedroom, slid out of my Ralph Lauren loafers and hopped in bed with just my under clothes on, and drifted off to sleep.

Nina woke me up to a kiss on my forehead. When I opened my eyes, she was hovering over me with the biggest grin on her face.

"What time is it?" I asked.

"It's twenty minutes 'til noon." She responded ecstatic.

"Damn, it's late! Where is my phone?" She handed me my phone off the nightstand, and I checked for any missed calls or unread text messages. "Well didn't nobody call me, so I guess everything's okay," I said as I lifted the sheets that covered my half-naked body and sat up. Nina followed suit and scooted closer to me. Anytime she was clingy I already knew what she wanted. "What's up, bae?" I asked her, even though I already knew the answer.

She hesitated and said. "Quay, you left me last night with a wet pussy."

That was my cue. I removed the covers that was wrapped around her body which revealed her pretty, shaved pussy. She spread her legs which made the view better and I dove headfirst in between them.

"Oh, shit, Quay," she whispered after inhaling deeply before planting her hands on top of my head.

I took my time as I gave every part of her pussy my undivided attention. I slowly sucked on her lips while giving her eye contact, before making me way to the clit. I swept my tongue across it slowly back and forth.

Her body squirmed in ecstasy as she began to arch her back. "Stop teasing me, Quay," she begged then wrapped her legs around my head. She was pulling my dreads so tight I thought my scalp would lift.

I wrapped my lips around her clit and began to flicker my tongue quickly back and forth. Her body jerked like she was having a seizure. She uncontrollably start grinding her pussy on my face. I moved my tongue in a circular motion which made her go crazy.

"Please, Quay, just fuck me!" She begged. I ignored her cries and continued to suck her clit. "I want you inside of me, now," she weakly pleaded.

I pulled away, lifting up on my elbows. "Fuck it. Go get him," I replied arrogantly.

She hopped out the bed and ran into the closet to retrieve my 8-inch strap-on dildo.

"Get in position," I demanded while I strapped the harness around my waist.

"I want you to make love to me." She said with a smile.

I took the head of the dildo and rubbed it against her pussy, teasing her as I gazed into her eyes before falling deep inside of her. I dug into Nina's pussy for at least thirty minutes. I had her in all types of positions while I danced and dug myself deeper inside of her.

"Quay! Quay!" She screamed. "Oh, Quay you feel so good! I'm cumming, I'm cumming!" She cried out into my ear.

Penetrating her alone made me bust, but I wasn't going to tell her that. You tell a bitch something like that and they'll run with it. Nina's body went limp and during that time an orgasm shot through my body. I pulled away as I lifted up and rested on my elbows, but kept the dildo still inside of her. I looked into her eyes and wiped the sweat from her forehead. She reached up and grabbed the back of my head and pulled me back down to her lips. We kissed slow and passionately. I pulled out and slapped the dildo onto the lower part of her stomach until all of her juices filtered out. I unstrapped the dildo and lay next to her. Sex with Nina was mind-blowing. I loved to please her. It was something about the way she looked and talked dirty to me while she put that pussy on me.

After all the touchy-feely shit was over we hopped in the shower. She washed my back and I washed hers. Her body was beautiful. What I loved the most was her perky breast. There was never a dull moment with her. After we got out the shower, we put on comfortable clothes to chill around the house in.

CHAPTER 12
MUN

I woke up to Donk standing over me with a blunt in his hand while Lil' Boosie played deafeningly on the laptop. We crashed at the spot last night. I guess with all the bullshit going on a nigga just passed out. I still couldn't believe what happened. I hate the idea of not knowing. Since then my mind has been everywhere. Since I been selling dope a nigga has never tested me. I puffed on the blunt and passed it back to Donk. At least his throwed-off ass was home. He's always on his toes— strapped and ready. Who would have thought a fine ass bitch like the one from the club could be on a mission? Nobody but Donk. I guess Quaylo did too. I chuckled to myself. She was something else.

"You good, nigga?" Donk asked with the blunt dangling from his lips.

"Yeah, I'm straight. Just thinking about a lot of shit."

"So, what time you want to meet up with ol' boy?"

"ASAP. Let me call him." I retrieved the phone from my pocket and called Lito. "Hello?"

"Wassup?" Lito asked.

"I'm ready. Where at?"

"Same place. In an hour."

"Bet," I said before disconnecting the call. I walked into the bedroom where Rico slept. He was sprawled out on the bed fully clothed with residue all on his nose. Nigga was getting sloppy and careless now. I just shook my head and closed the door, disgusted at the sight of the nigga.

"Aye, take me to mamma house so I can get myself together." Donk said standing in the middle of the hallway, holding the crotch to his denim shorts while rubbing the back of his head.

"Come on," I replied, grabbing my keys and phone off the table. "Rico, we gone." I shouted before I closed and locked the door. "Make sure that nigga up," I demanded to Lil' Tim who stood on the curb with a small group of goons.

The entire drive to Rochelle's house, my mind wandered non-stop. What if someone in my circle set me up? If so, the only people outside of my blood that knew about the pick-up was Rico. Betrayal never came to my mind with Rico until now. Drugs will make you do shit you never thought to do before. Or was it an enemy that was watching me the whole time in the club and was waiting for me to leave? It had to be robbery, because if they wanted me dead, they had more than enough opportunity to kill me.

My cell phone began to ring. I snatched it from my pocket and looked at the caller ID. I didn't recognize the number, so I hesitated to answer it. But then I decided against it. I figured it might just be someone important. "Hello?" I answered.

"Mun?" The female caller asked.

"Yeah?" I responded curiously.

"Hey, baby, this Bre!"

"Damn, what's up, girl? When yo ass coming back?"

"I'm leaving now. I had to use my mother's phone, and mine doesn't have any signal."

"Oh, okay. That explains why I didn't recognize the number."

"You miss me?"

"Of course, I miss you. Guess what?" I paused. "I'm in the car with my brother. He came home yesterday."

"Damn, baby, that's great!" She screamed into the phone. She seemed more excited about it than me.

Since the beginning I've always told her and expressed to her about Donk. We laughed and reminisced the whole ride to Rochelle's house. I ended the call before I got out the car. Donk had a puzzled expression on his face.

"That was Bre. The little chick I been fucking with for two years. The same one I was telling you about." I informed him.

"Oh, okay," Donk responded while unlocking the door.

The house was empty. Rochelle must have gone to church. She got drunk, smoked weed, and cursed like a sailor, but she made sure she was at that church house as my grandmother would say.

I sat on the sofa and pulled out my phone, sending a text to Bre. I ain't gone lie, I missed my bitch. It's not even about love; it's the level of respect. The courtesy and royalty she handles me with. I cut all my other hoe's off, my money was getting long, and I knew that's all they wanted, so whenever I do decide to dip off and fuck with another chick, it's just to get my dick wet and keep it moving. Shit, if Bre knew that she would kill a nigga.

Bre was the classy type, but she was hood too. She was a bit expensive, but I wouldn't have her no other way. She was just a lady with self-respect and morals. After Donk finished getting dressed, we headed out the door to go meet Lito.

Ah'Million

CHAPTER 13
BRE

As I exited the freeway, all I could think about was Mun. It's been three long weeks and I missed his sexy ass. The day of the funeral, my mom was really going through it. She wasn't speaking to no one or eating anything. All she kept repeating was, "God, why? Why did you take my little sister?" I didn't know how to respond or console her. I'd never seen her so vulnerable. She's always so robust and enduring. I hated seeing her so down. The drive back from the airport was extremely quiet. I tried cracking jokes here and there, but she didn't budge. I had a lot on my mind as well.

After two years of being with Mun I was finally ready to come clean. He deserves it, but it's so hard. *What if he decided to leave me? Or what if he feels like I lied to him,* I thought. A few weeks ago, I visited an Adopt-A-Child site, yet I still haven't made a decision on which child I wanted to adopt. Sadness slowly came over me, as I began to think about the chance of having my own child.

When I was seven years old, my babysitter raped me. The crazy thing is, my babysitter was my twenty-one-year-old boy cousin; his name was Lionel. My mom went to work. The five days he watched me was a nightmare. Lionel was more like one of those distant relatives. He rarely participated in any of the family activities and you hardly seen him at any family gatherings. He was just the only one available person at the time. My mom figured he was responsible and reliable, because he had a college degree, but he did more than feed me and put me to bed. I tried running, screaming, and fighting but nothing worked. The pain was inevitable. I never allowed him easy access so he always forced himself inside of me, which only made it more painful. It felt as if he was ripping my flesh with every thrust. I cried and cried, but no one heard my cries.

To this day I hate my dead ass father, because he should have been there for me. He should have saved me, but he didn't give a damn about me; not even a bitch that looked like me. My cousin threatened to kill my mother if I ever spoke a word to anyone, so I kept quiet. I never understood the true definition of the word "kill". All I knew was that it meant she'll be gone forever, and I'll forever have to deal with my cousin.

The only thing that saved me was that my mom lost her job.

At the age of nine my mom started doing home healthcare. Her first day on the job I begged to go with her. She was taking care of a patient named Ms. Lula. I loved Ms. Lula. She reminded me of my grandmother. She treated me like her own and showered me with gifts. From that day forward she fell in love with me and asked my mom to bring me to work with her from then on. I cried my eyes out when Ms. Lula passed away from a heart attack a few years later. Since that day, I hadn't seen my cousin. A few years later he got sent to prison for dating a minor. The girl was sixteen years old. When my mom got wind of what happened she was pissed. Rumor has it the girl lied and told my cousin she was eighteen, but I wasn't a bit surprised, 'cause I knew his MO.

After being sentenced to twelve years in prison, he got shipped to a maximum-security unit, where he began getting raped and bullied. He would write home and the family came together as one and contacted the warden and the NAACP, but I assumed nothing happened, because a few months later the warden contacted his mother and informed her that Lionel committed suicide. I guess he couldn't endure it any longer. I buried my secret, because in the end, before he left this world, he felt exactly how I once felt. Only difference is he wasn't strong enough to endure it.

When I was sixteen my mother took me to the doctor to get my first check-up. She was astonished when she found out my fallopian tubes were scarred. She was also hurt when she found out my chances of being able to reproduce was slim to none. Despite the reasoning being caused by something that happened years ago, she continued to rant and rave once we got home. Not being able to hear her screams any longer I came out and told her the truth, and the reason I had kept it from her for so long. She was hysterical. If my cousin was still alive my mother would've walked to the prison and killed him with her bare hand. She wanted to call my Aunt Lauren whom was Lionel's mother and fight with her, but I calmed her down and talked her out of it. There was no one to blame.

Me and my mom were close since the beginning. It's always just been us, but after revealing that to her, it made our bond inseparable and we both made a vow to never keep anything else from one another. She was the one who convinced me to tell Mun. She figured eventually he is going to want to settle down and have kids. I hate the fact I couldn't have my own kids. Every woman's dream is to have a beautiful child when they're ready and willing.

Now I'm left to adopt someone else's. One woman's trash is another woman's treasure. I believe everything happens for a reason, and maybe I'm saving a child that's in the same situation I once was in.

"Ma, you hungry?" I asked while turning the volume down on the radio.

"No, baby, I don't have an appetite," she replied with tears in her eyes.

"Mother, it's going to be okay. You can't allow this loss dictate your mood. Death is a part of life. It's something we can't control."

She smiled and said, "I know, baby. I'll be alright. Like my pastor once said, 'God does not take you deeper to drown, he just knows your enemies cannot swim'."

I smiled and slowly nodded in approval as I headed back to Dallas.

Ah'Million

CHAPTER 14
DONK

After me and Mun met up with Lito, he took the birds to the spot, then dropped me off at Rochelle's house. I was laying on the sofa, eating pizza pockets when I decided to hit up Persuasia.

"Hello?" she answered.

"What's up, shawty? This Donk," I replied, still chewing my food.

"Oh, hey, boo. I'm glad you decided to call." She replied ecstatic.

"Yeah, something came up last night."

"Yeah, with ol' girl I saw you leave with?"

"Damn stalker. Look, let me take you out later." I smirked.

"I guess. What time you going to pick me up?"

"I'll be there around six. Send me the directions."

"Okay. Bye."

I pressed the *End* button and continued to eat my food. On the low the little incident from last night had me thinking twice about moving fast with these females, but I can't help it. For six years I was surrounded by niggas. Shit, I'm just trying to change the scenery.

"Boy, get your feet off my damn table!" Rochelle yelled, walking through the door with her grocery bags in her hand. The beads of sweat glistened off her nose as she walked past me smiling. "Where was your ass last night?" She asked putting the groceries in the cabinet.

I walked into the kitchen where she was and began to help her. "We left the club late, so I spent a night at Mun's." I explained.

"You better not be lying, nigga, and you better start using protection with them fast ass girls."

"Now, mama, what did that have to do with anything we was just talking about?"

"Boy, I wasn't born yesterday!" She raised her voice, and placed her hand on her hip. I just laughed to myself 'cause she knew exactly what she was talking about. That lady knew me just like the back of her hand.

When I was younger, I had a childish but selfish way of thinking. I used to think my mom showed favoritism to Quaylo because she was the oldest and only girl until I sat back and observed. When we were younger, we all attended George F. Winston Elementary. We wasn't as fortunate as most of the kids, and because of that we were picked on a lot. Now that I think back, kids can be so careless and cruel. The difference between us and most kids, we didn't take no shit. Even at a young age we didn't give no free passes.

If you talked shit you would get your ass beat and you better pray we didn't jump you. We transferred from school to school as we changed areas, due to the fact my mother couldn't keep up with the house payments, but what I did notice was every time we transferred Quaylo had a different book bag. I hated the cheap mesh bags, but my mother would buy us one every year, because the other ones were too expensive. However, I used to feel some type of way, 'cause Quaylo had all pink ones with designs. I felt like it was unfair, and I just didn't understand, until one day we all got picked up from school. Rochelle was in her little red hoopty, a Toyota Corolla to be exact, when we all took off running to the car.

"Momma, I almost got caught," Quaylo said nervously, jumping into the passenger seat.

"By who?" My mom asked her with a wide-eyed expression as if the news shocked her.

"By her, mom," Quaylo responded while pointing at the lady standing on the other side of my mom's window.

Ms. Davis, our principal, tapped her finger against my mother's window to get her attention. My mom looked at Quaylo then rolled the window down to talk to the principal.

"My name is Ms. Davis and I'm the school's principal. What is yours?" She asked.

"How you doing, Ms. Davis? My name is Rochelle. Is there a problem?" my mom responded.

"Well, actually, there is. How much sleep does your child receive on the daily basis?"

You can tell the question caught my mother by surprise with the expression displayed on her face. "Ummmm… She goes to bed every night at 8 p.m. On Monday nights at 9 p.m. when they watch UFC. Why does her sleeping arrangements matter, Ms. Davis?" My mom asked.

"Well, today, I found your daughter laying right outside the freezer in the cafeteria sleeping when she should have been in class," Ms. Davis said. The statement shocked us all.

"So, wait, you're saying she was skipping class?"

"Yes. When I asked her why she was so tired, she said she didn't get any sleep last night and she was tired; she had to get a few hours of sleep, which she knew would be impossible to do in class."

"Well, Ms. Davis, last night me and her father got into a heated discussion that didn't last long, but once she was awake, she probably couldn't go back to sleep. Therefore, her lack of sleep is my fault. I apologize and it will never happen again."

"Thank you, Ms. Rochelle. No discipline will take place. I was just a little concerned, but thanks again for your time."

"You're welcome." And with that said my mother drove off.

"See, mama, I was trying to tell you that when I was in the freezer, I heard someone come in so I hurried and zipped my book bag and closed the freezer, and curled up into a ball like I was asleep. A few seconds pass and I hear voices. That's when Ms. Davis tapped me and I squinted and yawned like I had just woke up," Quaylo said.

My mother looked at Quaylo with guilt and defeat in her eyes.

"I still got the food, mama. I got ten chicken patties, ten burritos, and a big bag of French fries," she retorted trying to lighten the mood.

"Baby, that's going to be the last time you take anything else out of that cafeteria. If she ever catch you in the act, she'll know this time was just an act and you'll be held responsible for all the missing food. I can't allow my baby girl to get in trouble, because

I can't make it out the struggle." The tears fell slowly down my mother's face and you could see the stress in her eyes and hear it in her voice. She turned and faced me and Mun. "Don't y'all ever lift your hands to steal anything. Work hard for what you want. Do better than me. don't put your families through the same shit," she expressed through clenched teeth as her bottom lip quivered and her tears fell freely.

All this time I never knew Quaylo was stealing food from the cafeteria. I knew things were rough, but I didn't know it was that bad. I immediately felt guilty for pouting over a materialistic ass book bag, when it was a reason behind it the whole time. Rochelle was just too ashamed to tell me the truth. It hurt me to the core to see a beautiful and independent woman so broken. Every tear she dropped made me hate my father even more. He never did shit but send jailhouse cards and write letters occasionally. He got sent upstate on a fifteen-year bid years ago for a drug charge when I was still in my mother's womb. Fuck that nigga. I wanted to help my mother so bad, and one day I did, and to this day I am.

My phone rung which snapped me back to reality. It was Rico. "Hello?" I answered.

"Aye, what's up, Donk? Mun told me to hit you up. I'm trying to get down." He said sounding a little nervous, if you ask me.

"Aight, cool. I'm setting something up right now. I'll call you and let you know the play a day ahead of time." I responded.

"Alright, bet."

I sat the phone on the table. I reached into my pockets and peeled off fifteen hundred dollars and placed it inside of Rochelle's purse. "Aye, mama, I'm about to bounce in a little bit but I'm coming right back." I said.

"Okay, baby. Bring me back a sack and a bottle of Moscato." She responded while putting the groceries up.

"Ma, between me, Mun and Quaylo, you do not have to drink this cheap ass wine." I laughed.

"I know, baby, but that's what I like."

"Alright," I said walking out of the kitchen. I was meeting up with Persuasia in a few so I guess I'll start getting ready.

CHAPTER 15
RICO

I finally was able to get in contact with Donk and now I'm on board. If I'm gone keep digging into my stash to support my habit I'm going to need more money from every angle possible, cause one thing I know for sure, I can't bite the hand that feeds me. Mun showed me love when my own blood deserted me.

Growing up, my mother was like having no mother at all. She left me at home all the time. No food, water, no nothing. I remember numerous nights I'll go open the refrigerator, and the stench alone would make me sick to my stomach. The bulb was always dim and I would have to squint just to see inside. The only thing that occupied the fridge was spoiled milk, a half-empty box of baking soda and a small container of butter. Most days I would rummage through the garbage and find pieces of meals my mother had thrown out, hoping it was enough to fulfill my hunger. Some nights I would just ball up into a fetal position and silently cry myself to sleep. I never saw my mother throughout the day. If I did, she was sprawled out on the sofa asleep. She used to taunt me over and over, telling me I was a mistake, but other than that, she rarely spoke.

A few years later, my mother passed away. She overdosed on Heroin. My Aunt Mary was my mother's oldest sister. I was well-fed and she was more attentive, but I know deep down she didn't give a damn about me. When I was fifteen, I attended T. Wimble High School. Mun and a few other boys were kneeling in a huddled, into a circle in the restroom, shooting dice, when Mun got into an altercation with one of the dudes. He stood to his feet and lifted his jeans and the other boys followed suit. Seeing that he was outnumbered, he smirked and prepared himself for the encounter. I made my way through the crowd and stood next to him, and we fought it out, five against two, until the security came and broke it up. Since that day, Mun and I have been boys. He looked out for me in more ways than one, and when Donk get knocked, Ms. Rochelle invited me into their home.

It's no way I could look my nigga in his eyes and steal from him. Hell nah, that's just not how I move. I'm a made nigga. Last night was a little hectic with Mun being followed and Donk getting shot at. I got a feel on who followed my boy. It all made sense.

After five minutes or so of contemplating on my next move, I picked up my phone and called Quaylo. "Aye yo," I said.

"What's up, Rico?" She asked.

"You busy, ma?"

"I'm a little tied up, but nothing major. Why?" She asked.

"Come see me for once." I stated. I could hear her giggles in the background.

"Come see you?" She repeated.

"Yeah, I need to see you as soon as possible, and don't make me beg. Just come fuck with me." I held my breath for her response. I don't know what it is this lil' bitch did to me, but she kept me looking for her ass with a flashlight.

"Alright, I'm on my way."

"Alright, I'll be waiting." I hung up the phone with the biggest grin on my face. It's been a minute since I made love to her and I felt like a kid going to Chuck E. Cheese. I was so damn anxious, I hopped in the shower and washed my dick. I didn't want to be smelling like yesterday's pussy.

The lil' bitch from the club was a freak, but couldn't no woman yet do me like Quaylo. Ever since our first little hookup a few years ago I been addicted. Shit, while she here, maybe we can put our heads together and figure out exactly who followed Mun and why. Shit was crazy, but I wasn't going to just stand around waiting. My thoughts were interrupted by a knock at the door. I already knew it was Quaylo. I was only supposed to take a five-minute shower, but I got lost in my train of thoughts. I hopped out the shower, grabbed my towel, wrapped it around my waist and jogged to the door.

Still dripping wet, I opened the door and couldn't help but to take in Quaylo's appearance. She looked so fucking sexy with her mini MK dress, matching MK sandals and her dreads were thrown into a messy bun. Her tight dress complimented all her curves.

"Are you gonna let me in, nigga?" Quaylo asked with her hand on her hip.

"Damn, my bad. I was just checking out your swag." I stood to the side and watched her as she swayed past me.

"Look, Rico, I didn't come for sex. We—" Quaylo had her back turned while she was giving the speech, but soon as she turned around and seen this dick standing at attention, whatever she was saying immediately ceased. She cleared her throat and put her hands on her hip.

"Now what were you saying?" I asked arrogantly while I stood there, rubbing the tip of my dick.

Quaylo wiped the sweat from her forehead. "I didn't say nothing. It's just a little hot, that's all," Quaylo said before she sat down on the sofa.

I slowly walked toward her and sat down beside her. "Come on Quay, you know what I want, and I know what you want, so stop playing." I whispered in her ear as I slid my hand up her dress and pulled down her panties.

"Wait," she whispered nervously as she grabbed my hand and looked me intensely into my eyes.

"What's wrong?" I asked.

She shook her head and said, "Nothing, bae. I'm just really feeling you, but I know your kind."

I paused and sat straight up. "My kind?" Her response caught me off guard and she could tell by the wrinkles in my forehead that I was slightly livid.

"Calm down. I'm just saying I'm okay. I'm living my life like it's golden. I sleep and eat good. Stress-free. All of the above. I just feel once I start going steady with you a lot is going to change." I let her go on and on, and while she expressed how she felt with words I began to express my feelings with my hands.

I pulled her panties to the side and before she could even stop me, I began to flicker her clit with the tip of my finger. Anything she was about to say turned into moans. She spread her legs apart slowly while I used my other hand to slide her panties off. I never been so anxious to fuck a bitch, but Quaylo turned me on in ways I couldn't explain.

She had the sexiest moan and sex face. I eased on top of her and used my knees to pry her legs apart. Her body was tense like she was afraid, but I didn't want to hear no sentimental shit at the moment, so despite her reaction I slowly slid up inside of her. She grabbed the pillows on the couch and bit down on her bottom lip. With every stroke I looked into her eyes as if I could see into her soul. I slid my hands underneath her ass and spread her butt cheeks apart and deep-stroked her slowly as I planted soft kisses on her forehead.

I was taken by surprise when I heard her say, "Oooh, I love you, Rico. I love you, daddy."

I know good sex make you say any and everything, but Quaylo never did that. With those words still in my head, I lifted one leg over my shoulder and picked up my pace. I was on the verge, but I had to hold on. I wanted us to cum at the same time, but as her body began to shake, I knew she couldn't last no longer. I slightly lifted up and fell back in the pussy with one last thrust. "Aaaaaarrrrrrrrggghhhhhh!" I roared while I clutched her trembling body at the same time.

We lay in the same position for a few minutes until I got the strength to roll over. I picked her fragile body up and carried her to the bedroom, where we had another session of mind-blowing sex. We lay with our bodies intertwined until we drifted off to sleep.

CHAPTER 16
MUN

Me and Donk sat in my navy-blue Ford Focus waiting on Lito to arrive. I went to the dealership yesterday and bought the plain yet subdued car. Whoever followed me is familiar with my ride.

"You talk to Quaylo today?" Donk asked me as he turned the radio down.

"Nah. Last night I did. Why? What's up?" I asked.

"I was just asking. Usually she'll hit a nigga up. Her little ass always busy." Donk stated. He was always so worried about Quaylo; obviously forgetting the fact she was grown.

"Nigga, you trippin'. Besides, she grown now, Donk. Chill out." I chuckled.

"Nigga, you already know how I am behind Quay." Donk said.

The three of us were tighter than vice grips. We all shared the same room up until middle school. Rochelle could never afford a three-bedroom apartment so we were always left to share a room.

Ring! Ring! Ring!

"Waddup doe?" I asked, looking around the empty lot.

"I'm in the third parking spot to the left." Lito said and ended the call.

"He here," I told Donk as I made a sharp turn and headed toward Lito.

He was in a black Chevy Durango. He passed me the black duffle bag through the window while eyeing Donk with a composed but flustered expression on his face.

"Wassup?" Donk asked.

I quickly intervened. "Aye, Lito, this Donk, my little brother, and Donk this Lito."

"No problem, Mun. I was just used to seeing the other cat with you, and it looked like I seen your little brother from somewhere. That's it." Lito said still eyeing Donk skeptically.

"I never seen you before, fam, but I know if you fucks with my bro you good people." Donk replied matching his gaze as he handed Lito the duffel bag of money.

Lito grabbed the bag and said, "Same time and location next week, little brother."

Donk smirked, sensing his sarcasm. He responded with a head nod as we pulled off.

"You good?"

"Yeah, I remember ol' boy now."

"Who?" I asked.

"Yo' connect. I robbed him years ago when he was just a worker. I can't remember the nigga name he was working for, but Big Mike plugged me in on the lick. His only request was that I keep it nice and clean since it was his own people he was plotting on."

"Oh, yeah? Nigga, I know you like the back of my hand. Soon as he said he knew you, I instantly figured you probably robbed the nigga." I laughed.

"I hope he don't remember, 'cause you got a nice little shop set up. I don't want to fuck that up for you."

"Shit, it is what it is, fam. Call Quaylo and tell her to meet us at the spot." I turned down the volume so he could hear while I proceeded to my destination.

"Aaaaaayyeee, meet us at the spot in twenty minutes." He said then ended the call.

After several turns, I finally pulled up at the spot. Today was like any other day. Ronnie was mowing the grass. Ronnie was an older addict that I've dealt with for years. He smoked crack, but he didn't let the drug dictate his honor or dignity. He was loyal and I liked that about him. Most addicts would betray any and everyone for a hit. After I parked my car I turned off the engine. I hopped out and nodded in Ronnie's direction.

Donk was right behind me with the duffel bag. "Damn, Quaylo got here fast." He said looking at her Challenger parked in the driveway.

Rico opened the door with a huge grin on his face, like he hadn't seen us in months.

"What you cheesin' for? I see you ass done woke up." I said brushing past him. I spotted Quaylo on the couch, smoking a blunt.

"Waddup doe?" She said, handing me the blunt.

"What's up? How long you been here?" I asked.

"I just pulled up." She shot back.

"Oh, okay. Tell me something." Donk interjected with a mug on his face.

"There you go. Boy, I told you I'm grown," she replied as she playfully punched Donk on the arm.

"I don't give a damn." Donk replied with a grin. He took a seat on the couch beside her.

I threw the duffel bag to Rico and headed toward the kitchen to make sure everything was set up. Rico began unloading the bricks and placing them on the table. What he didn't know was that I was paying close attention. I could tell he was using when I noticed how his eyes swiftly scanned the dope and the beads of sweat that formed across his forehead. I shook my head in disgust as I continued to eye Rico from across the way.

"A nigga on Eighth Street want a whole thang, so I'm gon' go put this up in the back. I don't want to accidentally whip it up."

"Donk!" I yelled out once Rico disappeared.

"Waddup?" He replied.

"I told you I wasn't tripping. That nigga out there bad, bruh, but for every gram he steal, that's how many holes I'm gon' put in his head," I said, walking out of the kitchen.

"You know I been itching to get his ass," Donk suggested.

"Nah, I'm gon' handle it. It's personal. Come on. Y'all ready?" I asked Donk and Quaylo.

"Yeah, drop me off at Rochelle's. I got a date." Donk stated.

"Alright, I'll link up with y'all later. I'm 'bout to duck off." Quaylo said.

"Bet," I responded, opening the door to leave.

"Don't be out too late. I'm taking you and momma to lunch tomorrow." Donk chimed in, wrapping his arms around Quaylo's neck playfully before going in separate directions.

CHAPTER 17
QUAYLO

I made it back to Nina's apartment, but there was no sight of her. The place was spotless as I spotted the plate of steak and potatoes sitting on top of the stove. I was going to call Nina to ask her whereabouts, but decided against it. Technically me and shorty wasn't going steady, although I really enjoyed her presence and consistency. That alone kept me around. I just can't see myself settling down with a stripper. I understand a girl got to do what she got to do, and a little pussy popping pays the bills, but every time I think about bagging the bitch, I reconsider. Now I'm not knocking the hustle, that's just not my preference. To be honest, a part of me wants Rico, but I know Donk will lose it. I know I'm the oldest and I do whatever it is I want to do, but since I was a kid I've always respected my brother's mind and wishes. Besides, Rico done got turned out on that coke and think a bitch haven't peeped the shit. I know if I peeped the shit, Mun has too. The sound of keys jiggling snaps me out of my thoughts.

Nina walks in with a few shopping bags and a huge smile on her face.

"Damn, big money." I said sarcastically.

She chuckled at my sense of humor while placing the bags down. "How long you been here?" She asked.

"About ten minutes." I stated.

"I think I'm gon' have that set up for us pretty soon."

"That's what's up. It's 'bout that time." I replied looking her up and down.

"Where you going?" She asked, eyeing me as I stood by the wall devouring my steak.

"I'm about to go chill with my momma for a little while."

"Okay. What time you'll be back?" She asked, low-key vexing my spirit.

"I don't know. I won't be out too late?" I assured, giving her a soft, wet kiss on the lips. I grabbed my purse and a Sprite out of the fridge before walking out of the door. I walked down the stairs and hopped in my Challenger, making my way to Rochelle's house.

It had been a minute since Rochelle and I spent quality time. The last time I sat and enjoyed her presence was Donk's first day out. When I pulled up to Rochelle's house, her porch was surprisingly empty. Usually, her and Rhonda would be sitting on the porch getting lit. I parked my car and killed the engine.

"Hey, baby!" She yelled from the front porch. She must have heard me pull up.

"Hey, momma," I replied, excited as I walked up to her and gave her a tight hug.

"What's been going on? Why your ass haven't called or came and seen?" She fussed.

"Mama, I been running around with Donk and Mun. I apologize, calm down. I'm here now," I assured, closing the front door before flopping down onto the sofa.

"Whatever. You never too old to get your ass whooped. Remember that," she babbled.

"Okay. Ma, I bought this new Kush from my Hispanic friend. It's called Green Crack."

"Crack? What?" She called out, looking at me over her shoulder.

"It's called Green Crack. It's weed, momma. Stay calm." I laughed. This lady was so dramatic.

"Oh, okay. Roll up. I'm gon' grab us a Daiquiris while I warm up this food I cooked earlier. Your brother lyin' ass supposed to been here." She regulated as she walked off into the kitchen.

I might just spend the night so I can surprise Donk when he get here. I missed the good old days, I thought. All of us under the same roof. It never was a dull moment. I remember Donk and Mun's first lick.

It was the first day of summer of the year 2008. Mun was 14 and Donk was 12. I had just got released from TYC, a juvenile prison, for burglary of inhabitation. I had been home for about a week, and despite me being away for those seven months, things at home were still the same. Rochelle was still struggling and fucking with this piece of shit ass nigga she called her boyfriend. The first couple of days I was excited to be a free woman and to be reunited with my family, but as my brothers began to complain and rub their tummies, I shook my head in disgust as I watched recaps of the same shit all over again. My mind begin to drift back into my old thoughts as I reminisced and dwelled on my old ways. As time passed, I tried blocking it out but every time I opened the fridge and it was empty, I flashed. Every time I realized I was wearing the same pair of shorts three days out of a week with only a different t-shirt, I flashed. With every bend of my flip-flops that made them look like banana peels, I flashed. And even though my family begged me to stay out of trouble, I couldn't help myself.

"I'd rather be in jail than to be broke," was my motto. My mind was already made.

Rochelle left for work at 5:00 a.m. By 5:10 a.m. I was going to be out of the house and on the lurk. I stayed up all night that night. I couldn't sleep. I watched the numbers on the clock change and it felt like it was taking forever for 5:00 to come. A few minutes later my momma did her usual routine and peeked in on us before going to work. I quickly shut my eyes as if I had been sleeping the whole time. She closed the door to my bedroom and then a few seconds later I heard the front door slam.

I hopped out the bed and ran to the window and peeked out the blinds to make sure she had pulled out of the driveway. I noticed it was still a bit dark outside. I put on my black uniform pants, black thermal top and threw my black book bag over my shoulder. I was lacing up my red and black Jordan's when Donk woke up.

"Where you going?" He asked.

"Over Rasha house." I replied dryly.

"You ain't going over Rasha house dressed like that. Stop lying, Quay."

"Man, lay down, Donk." I paused, looking him dead in his eyes.

He stood to his feet and tapped Mun a few times on his legs to wake him. "Quaylo trying to go hit a lick." He snitched.

"No, you ain't going nowhere. You just got out." Mun stated yanking the sheets off his body as he stood to his feet with sleep still in his eyes.

"You can't go back. Let's us go. You was gone too long. No telling how much time you'll get if you get caught a second time." Donk stated with his chest out.

"Hell nah. What if y'all get caught up? Fuck that. This shit ain't for y'all. Chill. I'm gon' be good." I assured with a mug on my face.

"Wel,l we going with you." Mun declared.

"Man, come on. Not right now, y'all. Just lay back down, please." I begged.

"Nope. Let's go." Donk said as he began to get dressed.

I knew it was a no-win situation. I just sat on the edge of my bed enraged as I contemplated my next move. They looked so innocent, yet determined. I hate we even had to discuss things of the nature. Why couldn't we have a life like regular kids our age? We supposed to be in bed asleep right now. I know once they go out there today, it's no turning around. Once you hop off that porch, it's a wrap.

I finally gave in. "Alright, y'all can go. Just, please, be careful. Don't be inside the house for too long, and if you get any type of funny feeling, just take off running. I'll be on the front porch waiting," I directed, regretting the words as soon as they parted from my lips.

"Bet," they replied in unison.

With that being said, fully dressed and a book bag on their backs, they walked out the room and headed out the front door.

When Donk reached for the knob, I grabbed his arm. "Look, I love y'all."

"Alright, Quay, let us go. We love you, too." Mun replied agitated.

Donk opened the door and I followed closely behind them and sat in the wooden chair on the front porch. They walked out the gate and headed down the street without even looking back. I rocked back and forth nervously waiting for they're return. I watched cars drive by and people of all different ages walk to the bus stop at the top of the street. Minutes passed and still no sign of Mun and Donk. I became impatient and hurried into the house and began to get dressed. While getting dressed I hear the front door. Mun and Donk walk in carrying a big plasma TV. I darted across the room to look out the front door to make sure no one had seen them before closing the door. I smiled at them and helped place the plasma onto the sofa. It was a 42-inch Sony flat screen.

Donk dumped out the things in his book bag. It was only a suede pink jewelry box. "This the only thing we found and all that shit in there fake. I just brought it to see if you wanted something out of it." Mun said.

"Well, at least y'all got this plasma. I can try and get two fifty for it, but for sure two hundred," I said.

"Okay, and you can have half of that," Donk stated, slightly disappointed.

"I don't need half, just give me forty dollars so I can buy a few groceries and a perm."

"Okay."

I searched through the jewelry box and Donk was right, it was all costume jewelry. "Yep, all this shit fake," I assured. You could tell they were disappointed by the looks on their faces. As soon as I was about to shut the box, I noticed another compartment. When I lifted it up, I saw an envelope, and not just a regular envelope. It was a bank envelope. When I pulled the money out, I noticed the hundred-dollar bill on top. "Here, y'all," I said as I handed Mun the money.

They both turned around, full of excitement. "Where was this?" They asked while Mun counted the money. "Four hundred and twenty dollars! Hell yeah!" They shouted in unison.

"So, once I sell the TV, that's like six hundred dollars altogether." I said.

We all split the money three ways and agreed to give Rochelle some money as well. Since that day, Donk and Mun lived the street life. It wasn't a time they left the house and returned empty-handed. Mun got older and start hustling, while Donk stopped looking for two-story houses and started looking for trap houses and stash spots.

Rochelle returned to the living room with two plates in her hand. Macaroni and Cheese, meatloaf, sweet potatoes and hot water corn bread filled the plate. I had already put fire to the Kush blunt. I passed it to her once she sat down and started devouring my food. I looked up at her while she was taking a toke from the blunt and couldn't help but notice the uneasiness in her eyes.

"Ma, what you thinking about?" I asked, concerned. She ignored my question and continued to puff the blunt without even looking into my direction. "Ma?"

She sat up, put the blunt out and gazed at me with tears in her eyes. Her look was so intense it sent chills down my spine.

"What's is it, momma?" I asked, sitting straight up, no longer comfortable on the sofa.

"Calm down, Quay... I'm alright, but it's something I've been holding on to for a long time and it's getting to me. Y'all my kids so y'all should know." She stated.

"Know what? Momma, what's going on?" I asked scanning her eyes for answers.

"I got sickle cell," she stated as the tears began to roll down her face. "If you don't know what it is, it's a blood disease."

Wrinkles formed on my forehead and my bottom lip begin to tremble as tears came to my eyes. "What?" I asked hysterically. I couldn't believe this was happening to me. My mother was like my best friend. We've shared secrets, laughs, cries. We've done it all. "I can't do this, ma. I can't do this. Please don't make me do it." I cried as I began to rock, choking on my tears.

"Quay, you the oldest, you're the strongest. When this shit kills me, you got to be there for your brothers." She said in a low, raspy tone. She reached over and wrapped her arms around me which only made me weaker.

"No. You leave, I'm leaving with you. I don't know a world without you. I can't live without you! My momma?" I erupted, completely overwhelmed. I felt like my world was crashing down. The pain was inevitable.

"Baby you have to know something that my mother use to always tell me and I want you to remember this, it's three things in this world that we can't control I don't care how hard we try it's impossible. People, past, and death. Everyone eventually has to die someday.

"I know I know but it's too soon for you ma." I whined.

"Quaylo! Stop it. I'm getting sicker with each passing day, the pain in my bones is becoming unbearable, but I don't want to be stressed on top of what I'm going through. This was something I couldn't avoid nor get rid of. I want to leave this world knowing you all are going to continue to be there for one another and stick together. It's just going to be you all, but for now, we all we got." She announced.

I squeezed my eyes shut tightly as I began to tell myself it was all a dream. I was always the strong one, but not this time. Every real man cries, but my mother needed me now more than ever. "Okay, momma. Okay. I'll be strong for us. I'll do it." I chanted, trying to convince myself. I wrapped my arms around her and hugged her like I'll never see her again. She was alive and breathing, and I swear I did not want to let go. I felt as if I held her and never let go then nothing will ever happen to her 'cause I know she's safe in my arms, but that was just a figment of my imagination.

"Quay, just promise me you'll keep the family together and Donk out of trouble. Don't let no one or no amount of money come in between you all. Stay tight like y'all were when y'all were young."

"Yes, ma'am," I stated in between sobs. We sat there for minutes. still holding each other and crying until there were no more tears left.

"Fire the blunt up," Rochelle joked, lightning the mood. I chuckled as she used her t-shirt to wipe away her tears.

"Does Mun and Donk know?" I asked curiously.

"No, baby, just you. I haven't had time to get all of you under the same roof, but I'm going to tell them this weekend when I invite everyone over for dinner."

We joked and exchanged neighborhood gossip. I even showed her flicks of females on my Instagram that should've been arrested for some of the shit they had on. We sat side by side, smoking blunt after blunt.

"Look, momma, I'm moving back in 'cause you never know when that day is coming. Besides, your days are numbered. I'm about to go pick up a few things and get the rest tomorrow," I stated as I stood to my feet.

"No, baby, I'm not handicap. Don't change your comfort zone, because of my issues."

"It's not that. I just wanted to be by your side every day until that day."

"If you insist. Be careful. Donk should be here by the time you get back."

I gave Rochelle a tight hug and kiss on the cheek before walking out the door. I put in my Yo Gotti mixtape and turned up the volume to his latest song, *Real Shit*. I instantly began to think about Rochelle as the tears fell from my eyes.

CHAPTER 18
NINA

I heard someone on the other side of the door fumbling with the locks. My heart began to beat rapidly, knowing it was no one but Quaylo. I'd been up waiting patiently for her to come home, before heading to the other side of town to check out this new club on 57th Street.

"What's up, bae?" She said dryly dropping her keys onto the table as she walked inside of the house.

"Hey, what's wrong?" I asked concerned as I leaded up from the couch and wrapped my arms around her neck. I could smell her Armani Si' Perfume. It was Quaylo's favorite scent.

"Nothing, ma. I'm just having some family problems and I'm gon' crash at my mom's for a couple of days. I came to pick a few fits up. I don't feel the drive to Eastside tonight." She replied pulling away from embrace.

Me and Quay didn't have a title, but I know the feelings are mutual between us. You could say this is her home. She was here more than anywhere else. I was really becoming emotional by the second to know she'll be somewhere else tonight.

"I hope everything's okay." I responded following her around the house as she picked through the clothes that hang on the rack inside the closet.

"Yeah. It's all good. Just hit me up, you got my number. I may stop through tomorrow or whenever." She replied nonchalantly.

Whenever? How long was she going to be gone? I wondered.

"Bae, hold on! I want to ask you something." I called out, stopping Quaylo in her tracks as she stood by the door.

Ah'Million

CHAPTER 19
RICO

I was on another level as I sat in my beige Lincoln Town Car watching the incoming and outgoing traffic in St. Middleton parking lot, parked directly across from the apartment building Nicki stayed in. I took my chances driving to her apartment, not knowing if she would be here or not, but due to the fact her Honda is here parked outside, that sums up everything.

I had Lil' Tim hold things down at the spot while I made my move. From the time Mun dropped those keys off until now, I've done snorted nearly a whole brick. The Tony had me feeling like I was the Incredible Hulk. Nicki was a fun girl, but I guess she's a set up bitch too and I don't condone bullshit of that sort, especially when it's my people involved. I wouldn't feel right knowing she's the suspect and sit back and not do or say anything about it. She might have some more cats in on the scheme. I don't know but I'm not going to wait, trying to figure it out. Weed smoke filled my Lincoln but that was just a cover up. My personal pack I brought along was nearly empty from the several bumps of cocaine I snorted. High as hell I began catching glimpses of myself in the rearview mirror. My eyes were buck and bloodshot red. The longer I sat, the more my mind played tricks on me. I put fire to the Kush blunt and reclined my seat to relax.

My lips grew heavy and before long I began to slowly drift off to sleep. The burning sensation from my left thigh is what awoke me. "Shit!" I yell as I quickly swat the blunt from my lap and onto the floor. I quickly grabbed my phone and used the light from the screen to locate the blunt, when I heard a car door slam. "Aaagghhhh!" I yelped out in pain, hitting my head on the bottom of the steering wheel, trying to quickly lift up to see who had slammed their car door.

To my surprise I heard the engine come alive and the back lights on Nicki's Honda lit up. I knew the blunt was somewhere underneath me. I stomped my feet multiple times in every direction to dislodge the lit blunt. I put my car in drive and slowly followed Nicki out of the apartments. I turned up the volume to J-Dawgs' *Behind Tint: Volume 2* mixtape as I discreetly trailed two cars behind Nicki. I could tell the direction Nicki was going. She wasn't headed to the club which was a bit odd. I saw a slight opportunity arise once she was on Dakota Street. She could've turned on any street better than this one. I quickly veered onto the street as well, picking up speed until I was directly behind her.

I picked up my .45 Desert Eagle that sat in the passenger's seat and aimed at Nicki's skull before firing six shots into her direction. After the back window shattered, the next shot hit her directly in the skull, instantly 'causing her to lose control of the wheel and crash into a parked car. I quickly hopped out my vehicle to make sure that Nicki was dead, but the faint sound of police sirens approaching caused me to dart back to my vehicle and speed off into the night.

CHAPTER 20
DONK

Last night with Persuasia was different. I figured she'll try to throw the pussy, but she didn't. Surprisingly she captivated me mentally with her conversation. She informed me that the only reason she waitressed at a club was to save up enough money to pay for medical school. Her dream career was to be a pediatrician. I'd only slept for a few hours while waiting on Quaylo, who was at one of her female friends' house laid up. But Rochelle was indefinitely sure that Quaylo should've returned last night. She was worried sick. Why was she so sure? Hell, if I know, but she was beginning to make me worry as well. When I arrived at Rochelle's last night, she explained to me that Quaylo left to get some clothes and she would be right back.

From the sounds coming from the kitchen I don't believe she slept at all. I eased out of my room and made my way to the kitchen. "Ma?" I called out.

She turned around looking like a raccoon by the eyes. Her eyes were red and puffy as if she'd been up all night crying. I was starting to panic, but in no way did I think Quaylo was in some sort of danger. "Something is not right. She's not even answering the phone." She replied, wiping the snot from her nose with the back of her hand.

"Ma, Quaylo is fine. Just give her another or hour or so." I replied as I guided her into the front room to take a seat on the sofa. The news reporter on the TV screen instantly caught both of our attention as he stood in front of a spot we were both familiar with.

"Reporting live from Channel Four News, I'm standing here in the Southwest area of Dallas on Dakota Street. We have a female victim who was shot multiple times several hours ago. The body is unidentified at the moment, but the victim was driving a black Honda Accord, 1996 model to be exact. If you have any information on what had taken place, please contact us immediately."

A sigh of relief escaped our mouths once the reporter stated the model of the car.

"Stay calm, you know Quay has a Challenger, and it's pink at that." I stated, not allowing Rochelle anytime to think negatively.

"Okay, baby, I know," she replied, looking straight ahead as if she was in shock.

"Hold on," I insisted as I quickly darted to my room to retrieve my phone. I called Mun as I stood in the middle of the room waiting for him to answer.

"Hello?" He mumbled, sounding asleep.

"Aye, do you know shorty's number that Quaylo fuck with?"

"No, but I know where she stay. Why? What's up?"

"Come scoop me, ASAP. Quaylo is missing," I stated before abruptly ending the call. I quickly shot a text to Jeff.

Jeff: As soon as the victim on Dakota Street is identified, text me the information.

I ran into Jeff while doing my bid. At the time, he was a lawyer representing my celly. I hired him as a private investigator, but he now works at the homicide building downtown.

CHAPTER 21
RICO

I had been up twenty-four hours straight. I figured once the drugs wore off I'd grow tired and drift off to sleep, but that wasn't the case. Instead I was wide awake, sitting on the sofa at the spot, paranoid as hell. The spot was jumping like any other day, but today my mind was somewhere else. The powder was starting to have its effects, and the effects weren't on the same page with my mind. I didn't like that shit whatsoever. I'm not going to bother telling Mun I handled the issue. Time will tell. It's not about brownie points or none of that shit, I just care about my family's safety.

The shooting incident had already hit every news channel in Dallas. Luckily, thus far they had nothing on the suspect. The sound of my phone distanced my focus on the reporter, but when I looked down at the screen, I got the shock of my life. *It can't be*, I thought. I stared down at the screen on the phone for what felt like hours until the ringing finally ceased. I began to sweat profusely as I swiftly looked around in every direction. Fear and guilt consumed my body and it wasn't long before my phone rang again. Only this time I just had to know who was on the other end.

"Who's this?" I answered abruptly.

"Boy thi—"

Before another word could escape her mouth, I unintentionally dropped my phone in shock and my jaw nearly fell to my lap when I heard Nicki's voice. I couldn't believe my ears. *If Nicki is alive, then who did I kill?* I asked myself as I stared straight ahead at the news reporter who stood on Dakota Street.

CHAPTER 22
NINA

I had been blowing up Quaylo's phone all morning so we could meet up. She never even called me once she made it to her destination. Last night was crazy, but I enjoyed myself. I couldn't tell her about the mad love I received at the club from niggas and bitches. My whole appearance screamed bad bitch. From the all-white spandex body suit to the gold Giuseppe Zanotti pumps, but what topped it all off was when I pulled up in Quays pink and black Challenger. Last night, before Quaylo left, I asked her if I could use her car to check out the new club on the other side. She didn't mind so we agreed to swap cars in the morning. I played it cool all night, not wanting to give an impersonator my time. Yeah, the dudes with the big, flashy but fake chains, and the fat bankroll, a hundred-dollar bill on top, but once underneath are ones. Those are the impersonators.

After hours of turning down nearly the whole club, I finally found the nigga I was looking for. His name was Sunny. He wasn't much of my type, but his money was. His diamonds were real, and he was flashy as hell, but his paper was long so he could do that. He ordered bottle after bottle. He kind of reminded me of Rico's stunting ass. Speaking of Rico, I hadn't heard from him since the day he rushed me out of the spot. I was ready to take his shit and be done with his ass. I reached over and grabbed my phone from the nightstand. I called Rico and patiently waited for him to respond. Quaylo was probably somewhere with a hangover from hanging out with her brothers all night. If she didn't love nothing in this world, she loved her brothers.

The phone rung six times before going to voicemail. I dialed the number again and on the second ring he picked up. "Who this?" He asked abruptly.

"Boy, this Nicki. You deleted my number?" I asked, astonished. Although Rico and I had plans to meet at the Hilton's Hotel tonight, he hadn't even called to make sure a bitch was still breathing. Maybe he's busy. It's cool. For sure tonight I'm gon' step in the Hilton's like I own the motherfucka. Confidence alone will attract a person's attention. That's how I captivated Quaylo.

She whispered in my ear one night at the club, "Not only are you sexy as fuck, but your confidence is sexy as well. You strutting around here like you bought the building." I smile every time I think about that night. She wore a Chanel letterman jacket, light gray tank top underneath her jacket, light denim Guess jeans, with a pair of black and gray Timberland boots. Her dreads were braided in two braids which made it easy to see her beautiful facial structure. Her long lashes made her eyes look chinky and her dark skin glistened from across the room. When I first walked past her, she did a double take, yet she didn't say anything. When I realized she wasn't going to speak up, I approached her with a friendly gesture and that's when she complimented my swag. We've been rocking since then.

"Hello? Hello?" I repeated before hanging up the phone. *What the fuck is wrong with him?* I thought.

CHAPTER 23
DONK

Mun and I wasted no time pulling into St. Middleton apartments. "She stay right up there in two-twelve," Mun directed, pointing toward shorty's apartment.

"There's Quaylo car!" I yelled, filled with excitement and relief.

"I told you Quaylo gay ass was somewhere laid up in some pussy." Mun chuckled.

We hit the stairs two at a time and knocked on the door.

"Who is it?" A female called out.

"Quaylo brothers," I responded.

She swiftly unlocked the door. "Hey, come on in," she said, opening the door. Shorty was gorgeous. Maybe after I talk to Quaylo I'll see what the status on her and shorty is, and if it's cool if a real nigga knock her screws loose.

"Tell Quay to get her ass in here," I stated before flopping down on the sofa.

"You Donk, right?" She asked politely.

"Yeah, why?"

"Y'all, I don't know what's going on, but Quaylo is not here. I haven't spoken with her since last night." She hesitantly stated.

"Since last night?" I questioned with a mug.

"She didn't seem like herself, but I didn't want to ask any questions, because technically that's not my place."

"What the fuck? Why the fuck haven't you called no one, when you couldn't reach her?" Mun interjected as he stood to his feet while pointing his finger in her face.

"So what car was she in, if her car is parked out there?" I asked nervously.

"She was in my car."

"And what kind of—"

Ring! Ring! Ring!

The room grew silent as my phone rung. I removed the phone from my pocket and noticed Jeff's name on the screen of my phone. I tried taming my shaky hands while I prepared myself for the inevitable. "Hello?" I answered in a low tone.

"The victim is twenty-six year old Shaquavia Richards."

I dropped my head in defeat as the tears came to my eyes. "You drive a black Honda?" I whispered to shorty, never taking my eyes off the floor.

"Yes," she responded, intimidated as she slowly began to back pedal.

I lifted my head, retrieved my Uzi that was tucked at the waist of my jeans and emptied the whole clip on shorty. With each shot, her body jerked like she was having a seizure before collapsing onto the floor.

"What the fuck? That was Quay?" Mun asked appalled. I didn't respond, I just stared at him with a cold expression. "What is it?" He repeated.

I began to lose all control, and before I knew it, I was some sort of untamed monster. Paint went flying across the room, glass plates and vases crashed into the walls. With all my might I kicked the plasma and sent it a few feet across the room. Before long everything was shattered into pieces.

"Donk, answer me!" Mun screamed from the top of his lungs. His veins protruded from his neck as he grew agitated with my silence. In all reality he knew the answer to his question. It was just too unbearable for him to believe.

I looked him into his eyes, matching his gaze. "She dead, bro. Quaylo dead," I stated in a shaky voice as I fell to my knees and sobbed like a baby.

Mun was hysterical as well. In all these years I never thought I'll be on my knees, mourning my big sister's death. Quaylo was precious. I was the ruthless one. Why didn't God take me? I only been a free man for a week, and someone done already murked my baby. I leaned against the wall and allowed the tears to fall silently.

"Why fuck with Quay, man?" Mun turns around and asks out of breath. The last I'd seen him so emotional was years ago when grandma died.

I reclined against the wall thinking of the "what if's" and "if only". But "*if.*" "If" was the case we'll all be rich. It was so many things we didn't even get the chance to experience together. I had already made plans to take her to Jamaica for her birthday. Since she was younger it was one of her dream vacations. *If* I hadn't been out cup caking with that bitch, I would've been at the house when she came over and would've been with her as well when she left to go get her shit. Pain pierced my heart when I said, "She'll still be alive if I would've followed her like she followed me that night."

"It's not your fault," Mun replied in a raspy voice.

"It probably wasn't my fault, but it was the truth. The question is, what am I going to tell momma?" With all the strength I had left in my body I lifted myself off the wall and went and stood beside Mun. "Look, fam, we got to go. The laws will be all over this place any minute now." I stated.

Mun lifted his head from the counter and more tears fell from my eyes when I saw his face. I never knew a life without my sister. Now I'm forced to live one. Even when I was locked up, I didn't feel a sense of loneliness 'cause she was always there, every step of the way. "Somebody in trouble, and I'm gon' get some answers," Mun spoke through clenched teeth.

"You already know it's blood for blood, but this not the place to mourn nor plot. Let's go."

Mun and I pulled up at Rochelle's house and I immediately noticed the marked police car in the driveway.

"Damn, I hate she had to find out like that," Mun stated dryly as we exited the vehicle.

We looked at each other and exchanged so many words without even speaking. With each step closer I became more and more depressed. Just so happens the officers were leaving. I could hear Rochelle's cries as soon as the door opened.

"I thought you were bringing her home? Please tell me these motherfuckers don't know shit and y'all found my baby!" She yelled. Rochelle was an emotional mess as she sat stagnant on the living room floor, wailing uncontrollably. She buried her head into her hands while me and Mun rushed to her side.

Seeing her so unendurable and fragile made more tears fall from my eyes. I squeezed Rochelle as tight as I could to let her know I understand.

"Aye, Donk, call your boy down at the homicide department." Mun called out.

Without responding I got up and walked to the back room where it was a bit peaceful and called Jeff. After placing the call to Jeff, I walked back to the front room and informed Mun on the little information Jeff had. "She was shot with a .45 Desert Eagle, and as of now no one saw anything. If he receives anything else he will let us know."

"Yeah, somebody saw something," Mun retorted.

"That's exactly what I'm thinking. Come on." I suggested.

"Where are y'all going?" Rochelle asked as she looked up with teary eyes.

"We can't just sit around and wait on them pigs. We got to do our own investigation. I promise we'll be back." I spoke with assurance before heading out the door.

The ride to Dakota Street was gloomy and silent. We both had a lot on our minds.

"Man, I hate to leave y'all again, but I got a feeling I won't be free for too much longer, 'cause somebody knows what happened to my sister," I mumbled.

"I know exactly how you feel. But we don't have to go about things that way. We can murk these niggas without a trace. I mean, Quaylo is gone, but you can't lose your life to the system again," Mun stated.

"You right. Well, we here. How do you want to do this?" I asked.

"Park right here. Let's start at the top of the street. You go left and I go right." Mun suggested.

"Bet," I said as we both hopped out and went into separate directions.

Out of all the people that stayed on the right side of Dakota Street, I only spoke to four. Some weren't home and some didn't bother to answer at all. Mun was talking to a Caucasian guy who resided in the last house on the street, so I continued to stand at the end of the street waiting for him.

"Find out anything?" I asked Mun as we both made our way back to the car.

"Well, everybody was saying the same thing, but the last dude gave me a description of the car. He said it was beige, and from the side it looked like it was a dude in the driver's seat," Mun stated, wiping the sweat from his forehead.

"A beige car? Damn, we didn't find any useful information. The people I talked to claim they didn't see anything, and the ones that did was stiff we already know. Can't no one even give us the model of the beige car?"

"Do you think somebody had a hit out for shorty?"

"Yeah, that had to be the case, 'cause I know Quay wasn't the target," I replied, hopping into the car.

"What's next?" Mun asked.

"I say we shoot up the apartments. That's the last place she was seen." I suggested seriously.

"Alright, bet. Maybe I'll feel a little better. Let's stop by the spot first." Mun said as I sped off Dakota Street.

A few days had passed since Quaylo's death and reality had really seeped in. To wake up and not be able to see my sister, let alone pick up the phone and give her a call. This shit was killing me softly. Mun and I paid a visit to St. Middleton the other night and laid down everything moving. Hopefully all the children was put away 'cause if it had legs and breath it was a target. Eight people were killed and twelve were injured, and Quay was still gone.

I have yet to eat or sleep. Everyone's a possible suspect in my eyes. Last night I was at the hood store on 8th and Corinth Street. I was walking out of the store when I noticed a guy pumping his gas. He was driving a beige Grand Marquis. I walked up on him and shot him right between the eyes. Jeff called me this morning and told me he knew it was me he saw on the tape, but he quickly got rid of it and the extra copy that was made.

Rochelle was going through it as well. I really don't know what's exactly going on with her, probably just a minor fall or minor incident of some sort, but her walk has changed, as if it's painful for her to take one step at a time. I didn't understand that shit. Quaylo's funeral, I wouldn't miss it for nothing in this world. I cracked a half smile as I recalled a time a few years ago before I went to prison. Quay was joking with Rochelle and said, "Momma, when I die, I want you to plat that *Bury me a G* by Young Jeezy." Who would've thought years later we'll be here today planning her funeral? I would've never thought she'll be the first to go. Mun and I paid for all the arrangements while Rochelle took care of everything else. I spoke with Mun earlier but for the past few days he's been doing his own thing, just like everyone else, doing whatever else, doing whatever necessary to maintain.

I got up from the sofa and headed to the restroom when I noticed a picture of Quaylo on the shelf. The picture was years old when she graduated from high school. "Man, I miss you so much, sis. I swear I'm gon' find the nigga that hurt you. If I was promised a spot in the Heavens right beside you, I'll take my own life. I'll die this second and leave it all behind. You my all, and without you, my all is nothing, and now I feel like I done lost everything." As the tear slid down my right eye, I told myself I wasn't going to cry anymore. I grabbed my phone and called Rico.

"Hello?" He answered in anticipation.

"I'm gon' swang by and scoop you tomorrow at eight, so be ready."

"Bet."

Before I ended the call, I thought about calling Persuasia. Since Quaylo's death, I haven't replied to any of here calls nor texts, but the longer I contemplated on doing so, I finally reconsidered.

CHAPTER 24
ROCHELLE

Days had passed and yet no suspect nor evidence has come to surface. As I looked in the mirror at my reflection, I couldn't help but to cry. Today was the day of Quaylo's funeral and I wish I wasn't here either, to tell you about it. I recalled when my mother used to say, "Rochelle, that girl look just like you." First my mother and now my baby girl. I missed my baby so much. Her presence alone was a blessing. She had the most alluring spirit. With all that has happened with Quaylo, I have yet to tell the boys about my disease. It's enough pain in their life already.

"Momma, you ready?" Mun shouted.

"Baby, here I come," I yelled back as I wiped my tears and walked out of the restroom. Although everything was paid for, other relatives had asked to pitch in, but I declined their requests. Besides, Quaylo wouldn't have wanted me to take the money anyways.

My boys looked so handsome. I tried hiding the depression, but Donk made it hard to do so once I stepped out the restroom and noticed his silent tears. He stood next to Mun with his head up and chest out. However, the confidence he presented, you would've never guessed he was in so much pain. He sported an all-black Ferragamo suit with Del Toro loafers. They were dressed very well; I just hate it was all for this occasion.

We hopped in my 2014 Buick Lacrosse and headed to the church. Quaylo's funeral was being held at Memorial Baptist Church on Mango Street. The ride to the church was quiet. There wasn't even any music playing. *Maybe now would be a good time to tell them about my current situation. I really don't want to. Life can be so unfair at times. Why should I have to tell my kids I'll be leaving this world soon? I know they are grown men, but how much pain should one have to endure?* I asked myself. *I don't know when exactly the Lord is going to call me home, but this shit really hurts when you know you're about to die.*

The pain in my bones was starting to become unbearable, and you could slightly tell in my walk. Both Donk and Mun had questioned me about the sudden change, but I brushed them off and lied, of course. I pulled into the lot of the church. A few cars had already occupied the lot. One of the cars belonged to my Uncle Joe. The funeral started in an hour. But it was few relatives already here. I walked up and greeted everyone while I went inside to help set up. Mun and Donk stayed back and conversed with Joe.

Minutes passed and the once empty site was now packed. I looked around the church at everyone that came to show their respects. You would've thought the whole city showed up. A few people had to stand because there was no place to sit. The church held a total of twenty rows; ten on each side. I noticed a couple of people smiling and hugging as if it was some sort of reunion, but right now I couldn't even force a smile if I tried. Me, Donk and Mun sat on the front row while I watched Pastor Hughes closely from behind my Chanel shades. I didn't want to talk, I didn't want a hug, I just wanted to get it over with.

"Man, I didn't know Quay knew all these people." Donk whispered to Mun as he removed his shades to get a better view.

"Hell, yeah. Everybody loved her lil' ass," Mun replied, taking a second look around the church.

"We are gathered here today for the celebration of the life of Ms. Shaquavia Richards." As the pastor continued to speak, tears fell freely from my face as I tilted my head backwards to prevent the tears from falling.

I felt myself getting weaker as I imagined Quaylo inside of the pearl tint casket. I closed my eyes and shut everything out as I began to pray for my baby because I knew she wasn't living right.

My prayer was interrupted when I heard my Aunt Rosy's angelic voice. *"I've had some good days and I've had some hills to climb. I've had some weary days and some sleepless nights."* Each word pierced my heart as I recalled her singing the same song years ago at my mother's funeral.

Reality hit harder than before and the sad tune only tantalized my broken spirit. Before I knew it, my shades hit the floor as I took off running toward Quaylo's casket. I weeped uncontrollably as I heard voices trying to calm my spirit. "Noooooo! God, why? Why my baby?" I yelled at the top of my lung while I held onto Quaylo's casket for dear life. My baby was gone and no amount of deaths, tears, nor prayer would bring her back.

CHAPTER 25
RICO

Earlier today, Quaylo's funeral was being held, but it's no way I could show my face and pretend like I don't know what really happened. It was as if I lost a part of me when Quaylo died. These past few days I've felt so lost and broken, to know I took someone so close to my heart, so close to my people, and it was all by mistakes. I love Mun like a brother, and lately it's been hard for me to hold a conversation with him, let alone look him in the eyes when I'm the triggerman behind his sister's demise. I thought Donk would suspect me off top. He never really liked me anyways, but when he called yesterday about the lick, I quickly pushed the thought out of my head. I'm glad the nigga didn't suspect me. His name been ringing bells in the hood on how he running around like a menace with a vengeance. Drawing down everybody that look like they knew something, and if he didn't like the answer you'd become another face on a t-shirt.

Yesterday, one of the elderly neighbors that gave the detectives the description of the accident after the suspect left the scene, came up brutally murdered. No one saw or heard from her in days, until one day one of her friends at the church got worried because she missed service and sent the police over. When I seen that shit on the news I just shook my head in disbelief, knowing one day I'd have to deal with that.

Lately Mun been kind of distant, but I can't even trip. I was still pushing the last of the dope I had left, but shit wasn't adding up; the numbers were off. I really needed this loot to add to the pot from what I had taken upon myself. I was content with the fact Mun not coming around as much. I needed the time and space to get shit right. I didn't want to duck and dodge him, but I damn sure didn't want to face him right now either.

Ring! Ring! Ring!

I looked down at my phone as Donk's name flashed across the screen. "Hello?" I spoke calmly as if I wasn't anticipating his call.

"Be ready, I'm on my way."

With that being said I began to quickly get dressed. I grabbed a pair of all-black 501 Levi's out the closet, and put on an all-black thermal shirt with my black and gray '95 Air Max. I put the black skully on my head and tucked my burner inside of my waist. I snorted two lines of coke and began to put everything up. It was no point of reaching out to Lil' Tim to hold things down, 'cause it wasn't shit to hold down. I chained the side door and locked all the locks before cutting the lights out so the fiends would know the shop is closed. I stood outside on the porch awaiting Donk's arrival, when I saw lights bend the corner. I don't know if I was nervous or uncomfortable but being around. This lil' nigga made me feel some type of way, and I don't know why 'cause I've never been bothered by another nigga's presence.

CHAPTER 26
DONK

"You strapped and ready?" I asked never taking his eyes off the road.

"Yeah, what the lick read?" he responded.

"Some Jamaicans own a bail bonds on Illinois Street, but my sources tells me they doing more than taking down-payments and collateral. They got some massive shit going on. I've been scoping the place out, before Quaylo died, but I got word tonight is the best night to make my move."

"Okay, how much we looking at?"

"Off top, a hundred and fifty grand, and that's just off what she heard, but I'm pretty sure it's more. Just follow my lead."

"Bet."

I parked across the street from the Quick & Easy Bonding Company. Shae had just sent word that her and the owner left to get a drink and she left the backdoor next to the emergency exit unlocked.

"Come on, we gon' hop the gate and go around back." I directed. Rico had been blowing up my phone ever since I promised him a piece of the action. I just hope the nigga 'bout what he be talking about. It was a quiet but busy area and that can be an advantage and a disadvantage. "Look, before we go in here, we going in together, we going to leave together. If something happens to go wrong and we get jammed up, don't mention my name." I stated looking at Rico directly into his eyes. I couldn't really read him, but I did know he was high off that shit.

After treading lightly past the buildings, we turned in the direction of the alley which led to the back door. I made sure my 9-millimeter was tucked inside my jeans, while my .40-cal rested in my holster before I approached the door. I slowly twisted the knob and opened the door. No one was in sight; just an old shelf with neatly stacked paper occupied the left side of the small space. I heard laughter coming from upfront so I slowly followed the direction of the voices with Rico trailing behind me. I instantly became disturbed when I heard voices in a different direction as well.

"What the fuck?" I mumbled underneath my breath, not knowing which way to go. I attached the silencer to my 9-millimeter. "I'm gon' go in blasting. You look for the loot." I whispered to Rico who nodded in agreement.

"What the fu—" Before the Jamaican dude could utter another word, I sent two bullets into his throat, silencing him forever.

Rico had his weapon trained on the other Jamaican that sat at the wooden table. The table was filled with stacks of money and all sorts of electronics. Rico rushed the guy, placing the barrel of his gun to his temple. "Don't say shit. Put the money in the bag." Rico spoke at a low tone as the dude slowly placed the money in the bag.

"How many of y'all' motherfuckas up in here?" I asked through clenched teeth.

"Fuck you, you poosey beetch. Find out on your own."

Psst! The shot hit him right between the eyes, before I was heading toward the door to do exactly what he told me. I waited for Rico to put the last of the money in the bag before placing one of the duffle bags over my shoulder. I quickly left the room. The voices I'd heard seconds ago could no longer be heard, which confused me. I looked over my shoulders and Rico was nowhere in sight. Before I could back petal into the room where I'd left Rico, gunshots rang out as bullets flew past my head.

Boc! Boc! Boc!

The dark vestibule area made it difficult to see what directions the bullets were coming from. I quickly dashed under a table to take cover. My eyes quickly adjusted to the darkness when I realized the bullets were coming from both directions. I swiftly fired at the gunman who wore a white t-shirt.

Psstt! Tsst!

"Fucking poosey boy!" he yelped out in pain before hitting the floor.

Boc! Boc! Boc!

Rico came out blasting like he was the motherfucking terminator with the duffle bag across his shoulder. "Aaarrrggghh!" Rico roared as he held his shoulder in pain. "I'm hit!" he yelled before diving behind a metal file cabinet.

"You won't meck it out alive!" The Jamaican shouted before turning the light switch on.

Click! Click! His once cocky expression vanished when he realized his clip was empty.

I rose to my feet and sent four bullets into his chest, causing him to collapse immediately. "Come on, let's go!" I screamed, taking the duffle bag from Rico and placing it on my other shoulder.

"Wait, it's probably more in the other room." Rico spoke though clenched teeth.

"Nah, fuck that. We already been in this bitch for too long. Shit didn't even go as planned; let's go!" I demanded, heading toward the exit whether Rico was behind me or not.

"Come on, Donk, we've already came this close. Just a few seconds is all I need to check the last room." He was convinced, holding his bloody shoulder.

"Come on, man," I mumbled while following him into the room. It was the last door on the left. I spotted all the surveillance and quickly destroyed all I could. To our surprise the safe was open.

Rico and I swiftly placed the stacks into the bag which nearly filled both bags. Rico tossed one bag over his shoulder while I did the same before exiting the room. We dashed down the long hallway. *I was sure to be set after this one*, I thought. As I reached for the door handle to the back door, the cool wind hit my face as soon as I stepped out into the night. Although Rico was wounded, he was moving like he never got shot. We bent the corner and darted across the parking lot when a multitude of Dallas Police cars swarmed us.

"Come on, nigga!" I yelled to Rico before dropping the duffle bags and jumping the fence.

Rico's shoulder wound slowed him down once he tried jumping the tall fence. He wasn't even halfway over before the policemen yanked him down by his jeans. I swiftly ran down the dark alley and tossed the gun inside someone's backyard before retreating back down the alley, only to run into a police car at the end. I turned around to run into the opposite direction only to be met by another police car. With nowhere to go, I placed my hands on top of my head in surrender.

CHAPTER 27
BRE

Me and Mun been ripping and running all day. I hate that all this shit is pouring down on him all at once. You could see the wear and tear in his eyes. I was trying to console him the best way I know how, but it was something I really needed to get off my chest, but why add fuel to the fire? Then again, will his nightmare ever end? I can't keep it from him forever. I have to tell him one day. Not today, I guess.

"Bre?" He called out with his eyes trained on the road.

"Yes?" I responded.

"What was it you needed to talk to me about earlier?"

My heart start beating fast as I battled with myself on whether I should tell him or not. With everything happening so fast I figured he would've forgotten. "Nothing, bae."

"You're not lyin' to me are you?" He stated in a cool, yet serious tone.

I exhaled deeply and stared at him for what seemed like hours before I opened my mouth to speak. "Mun," was all I managed to utter before the tears fell from my eyes while my bottom lip shook uncontrollably.

For the first time Mun took his eyes off the road to glance at me. "What's wrong? Just tell me. You can tell me anything." He spoke with a concerned but curious expression.

"Mun, you know I love you and I'm sorry I've kept this from you. I just didn't know how to tell you, 'cause I was afraid of how you would react."

"What is it? I'm not going nowhere."

"I can't have kids!" I yelled hysterically as I began to sob.

"What?" Mun asked while he stared at me.

"Mun, I just—"

Beep! Beep! Beep! The cars honked as Mun intensely watched me, diverting his attention from the road.

"Mun!"

He quickly grabbed the steering wheel and swerved to the left lane just in a lick of time. My heart was beating at a rapid pace; I'd never been so close to death. After Mun regained control, he asked, "How long have you known this? And why can't you have kids?"

"Mun, I'm sorry for not saying something sooner, but just know it took everything in me not to tell you. Since I met you I wanted to tell you, and once I fell in love with you I felt like I needed to tell you. When I was younger, my older cousin raped me every day for two years straight, and when I was fifteen, I found out my fallopian tubes were scarred, which made my chances of having kids slim to none."

Mun remained silent while he kept his eyes fixed on the road. I could tell by the way he squinted that he was in deep thought. I was hoping like hell he wasn't going to leave me, 'cause I really did love this nigga more than life itself. One thing I do know is real people recognize real shit, and I know he understands the daily struggles of life. Everyone just isn't able. "So, how is it you been my bitch for two whole years and you never told me this? Is that nigga still alive?" Mun asked in a calm but demanding tone. It was something about the tone of his voice that made my pussy wet.

"Mun, I was ashamed and afraid that you would leave me, because I wouldn't be able to give you your own seed. As for my cousin, he committed suicide while he was imprisoned years ago."

"Look, ma, I know shit happens and I really can't be mad. Yeah, I'm hurt. I would love to have a child by you— you're beautiful inside and out— but I ain't going nowhere. Will I get another bitch pregnant? Eventually. Bre, I'm a D-boy. I never know when my day gon' come, and I want a little Mun to continue the legacy. Don't start crying and hollering 'bout I'm cheating, 'cause if I ain't cut you off by now, then I'm not."

"Okay, baby," I said, wiping the tears from my face, smiling. *Ring! Ring!*

Mun pulled his phone out his pocket and answered it. I could tell it was his mother asking about Donk, 'cause he lied and told her he was out of town. I would've lied to my mother too if she was going through what Rochelle was going through.

CHAPTER 28
DONK

Back at square motherfucking one. I just got out of fucking prison, but really, I can't be mad at no one but me. I kept replaying the scene over in my head, and honestly, if it wasn't for Rico's greedy ass, we probably would've gotten away. I know them boys could've been sitting out there the whole time. If so, they would've been came in when they heard the first round of gunshots. It's a time thing, and if I would've just went with my first mind I wouldn't be sitting here. I'm here on some charges way more serious than last time. They booked me and made me change into these dusty black and grey scrubs. Now, I'm sitting in this holdover cell, freezing to death. I've been waiting for damn near forty eight hours just to go upstairs. I haven't seen Rico since they cuffed us and put us in different squad cars.

"Richards!" The officer yelled while he unlocked the cell.

"Yeah," I responded, squinting as the light from the other side seeped in.

"Gather your belongings. You're going upstairs," he said.

I picked up my court papers and tissue before walking out of the cell. I couldn't believe I was back in Dallas County. I just hope Mun have me out before Rochelle finds out. I hate breaking my promises.

We got off the elevator on the sixth floor. "You're going to floor number eight, make that left and go around the corner. Grab you a green mat before you go in." The CO said.

I had already known the routine. I picked the thickest mat out of the bunch, sprayed anti-bacterial spray on it, before wiping it down and heading to the tank. As I rounded the corner, I could see niggas in the window trying to see who I was, and when they realized it was me, they start hollering my name at the top of their lungs, but I didn't feel all of that. Soon as I walked into eighth tank, I couldn't help but to notice how quiet it was. I immediately began to look for an open cell to sit my shit in. I sat my things down inside of a cell on the bottom row with an empty top bunk, and rushed to the phone. It was only a few people in the dayroom, maybe because it was still a little early. I could tell the time by the television show. Maury and Jerry Springer was part of my daily routine last time I was here, the closest thing I got to seeing strippers and violence.

I let the lady on the automated system go on for what seemed like hours before the call processed.

"Hello?" Mun said.

"Aye, what's the plan?" I asked

"I got Steve working on a court date for a bond reduction, but first an examination trial to see what evidence they have, but regardless we gon' make somethin' shake."

"You talk to mama?"

"Yeah. She asked about you a few hours ago."

"What she say?"

"Have I heard from you. I told her you went out of town, and you'll be right back."

"Okay, bet."

"Hold on. This Steve texting me. He got the court date set for tomorrow at nine in the morning." Mun assured.

"Hell yeah! 'Preciate you, fam. Have you heard from Rico?"

"Not yet."

"Alright. I'll see you tomorrow."

"Bet."

After I hung up the phone with Mun I began to think about Rico. I wonder why I haven't seen him or why hasn't he tried to reach out to someone. I walked back to my cell, placing my mat on top of the bunk and laid down. It was some older dude asleep on the bottom bunk. I just hope he stay in his lane for the next twenty-four hours, 'cause I don't mind smashing a nigga while in in this bitch.

A few hours later I awoke to a lot of commotion. I lifted my head and saw a few nigga huddled up into a circle, shooting dice. I laid back down and closed my eyes, but I couldn't go back to sleep. My mind was all over the place. I looked toward the crowd and the first person I spot, kneeled is my homeboy Black.

He never took his eyes off the prize. Every time he rolled the dice, he'll say something then snap his fingers. "Stanky store!" Snap! "RIP lil' Quaylo—"

Before he could even snap his fingers, I rushed him, hitting him with two uppercuts to the chin that instantly dropped him, knocking him unconscious. I got on top of him and connected two more times to the jaw, waking his ass up.

"Aye, man, what the fuck?" Someone behind me yelled.

I quickly turned around like a deranged man and stood to my feet. "Wassup?" I yelled. "If any nigga got a problem with me beating this nigga ass, then come holla at me!" I turned back around and spat on Black before heading toward my cell. Yeah, we was cool, but he don't know Quay like that to speak on her name. I play about a lot of things, but she ain't one of them.

A few male guards quickly rushed in like some jump-out boys. "What the fuck going on?" The sergeant yelled. He wore a black collar shirt and green pants.

I just laughed at the nigga. If only I was out, I'd off his punk ass and send nothing but his name tag to his wife and kids.

"What happened to him? Who the fuck did this?" He yelled, making his way through the crowd to get a closer look at Black, who sat on the stool trying to regain his composure. No one said nothing and began walking toward their cells. "Oh, don't nobody want to talk?" He spoke looking around curiously and angry. "Come on." He said grabbing Black by the arm. "The rest of y'all rack it up! It's gon' stay like this until I get some answers!"

"That's some bullshit," a couple voices called out.

I headed back to my cell, not giving a damn if I was racked up or not. I climbed on top of my bunk and stared at the ceiling before drifting off to sleep.

Ah'Million

CHAPTER 29
ROCHELLE

I had been out all day shopping for summer dresses. Five stores later and I only found two dresses. Shopping was so much easier when Quaylo was alive. I spoke to Mun earlier and he informed me on Donk's whereabouts, so I guess I'll skip dinner with the boys and hang out with Rhonda's crazy ass. That's if I'm able. The pain in my legs has been ongoing for the past couple of days. I really didn't feel like hanging out, but you never know when you'll need days like this. I pulled up to my house and dialed Rhonda's number.

"Wassup, girl!" she shouted into the phone.

"Where you at?"

"I'm at the house. Where you been?"

"Bitch, don't worry about it. Just come outside." I hung up the phone.

Rhonda walked out a few minutes later with a Bud Ice in her hand and walked over to my car and climbed into the passenger's seat. Me and Rhonda been friends for a long time. She's been staying two houses down from me for years. she's more like a sister. She attends every family gathering and activity. "So, bitch you been shopping?" Rhonda asked with one of her eyebrows raised as she looked around in the backseat at the shopping bags.

"I did a little something," I replied with a smirk. I want to see the expression on her face later when I pull the dress out I bought for her. I couldn't help but to wince at the sudden sharp pain.

"You alright, Rochelle?" Rhonda asked concerned.

"Yeah," I responded, dragging my words while deeply exhaling.

"Talk to me, Rochelle."

I stared into Rhonda's eyes, and the tears slowly began to fall, grazing the top of my lip.

"Rochelle!" She yelled, looking saddened and puzzled.

The tears continued to fall, but if I had to rate the pain I was in on a scale from one to ten, I would have to say a ten. No one knew

119

my struggle, but my mother and Quaylo, and they were both dead and gone. "Rhonda, I'm in my final stages of my disease."

"Disease? What are you talking about?" Rhonda replied hysterically.

"I have sickle cell-anemia."

"Wha…What?"

"My last visit to the hospital, the doctor told me I had a small blood clot in my vessel, and as time passes the clogs expand which eventually become large enough to block my blood flow. It also causes pain in my bones, and right now the pain in my legs is unbearable. I just feel it, Rhonda, and I've been trying to sit my boys down and talk to them, but something always comes up."

With crocodile tears in her eyes Rhonda slowly drops her head and mumbles something I can't understand. "You my best friend, Rochelle. What am I going to do? You dying? Really?" Rhonda was looking at me with a pleading stare while her bottom lip trembled.

I could see the hurt and distress in her eyes, but it was nothing I could say to soothe her soul or mend her broken heart, so I just looked off into the opposite direction and allowed the tears to fall freely. Since teens, me and Rhonda discussed our future and how we'll plan and attend each other's weddings, and always be there for one another, but we never discussed this part of the plan.

"What am I going to do without you? Who I'm gon' call, talk to and kick it with? You all I know, Chelle." Rhonda said.

"Rhonda, if I had a choice, I would choose life, but eventually death comes to us all, baby. Some quicker than others." I assured while wincing from the pain.

"You're in pain?"

"Yes, and I think I need to go to the hospital."

CHAPTER 30
MUN

Today, Donk's hearing for his examining trial was being held. It was a few minutes after eight, and Bre and I sat side by side in the back of the courtroom. I was nervous as hell, knowing this could either go two ways. Despite the fact Donk assured me no one got killed, I know my brother. A body was just a body in his eyes. I just hope he was telling the truth.

"Hey, he's in a holding cell waiting to be called. I'm getting everything together and contacting my people in higher places." Steve said before walking back out of the small courtroom. I sat there in deep thought, wondering how disappointed Rochelle would be if she knew what was about to take place. She knows once a hustler, always a hustler, but I'm running shit so smoothly. I just can't figure out why Donk won't just put the tool and mask down and do something different because shit like this is going to eventually happen.

Rochelle never liked the life Donk chose. All she ever wanted was for him to change things up.

"Baby, do you think Donk killed someone? Bre whispered, obviously as nervous as I was.

"I don't want to talk about it, ma." I trusted her but not with everything. If I did trust her completely, it would be with my business, not my brother's. People changed and switched up every day. You see the bitch is just now telling me she can't have kids. My thoughts were interrupted when the D.A. and the clerk walked through the door. I guess it was almost time. I still hadn't heard from Rico, which I found very awkward. He was locked up a few months ago for a misdemeanor possession charge and I had to power off my phone to keep the nigga from blowing me up. I know life can be a bitch and full of surprises but I'm not ready for Donk to be a victim of the system again. Steve entered the courtroom; he wore a burgundy and olive-green Armani suit with a pair of burgundy and gold Tom Ford loafers.

"It's time," He said marching down the aisle. The judge came in as well and I began to loosen the tie on my cream-colored Gucci suit. My palms were sweating as I became somewhat nervous. Donk entered the courtroom in shackles. He looked at me and winked as I nodded in return.

"The State of Texas versus Dontrail Richards." The judge announced. As soon as the judge banged the gavel, the D.A. wasted no time informing the judge on Donk's past criminal history. He even went to the extent of unveiling his juvenile record but with everything he threw out, Steve had an even better comeback. I just shook my head as both the men continued to go back and forth.

"Your honor, my client was charged with Murder, but as you can see the weapon that matches the cartridge casing was never found on him, his co-defendant, nor the scene." The judge looked at the D.A. for a response, but not a single word was spoken.

"Wait your honor, no, the weapon wasn't found but we do have a solid proof that a robbery and murder took place. We have Mr. Richards and another suspect in custody that we arrested at the scene." The D.A. spoke, not wanting to give up so easily.

"We're dismissing the Murder charge until proven guilty. The Aggravated Robbery still stands and bond is set at $25,000. Meeting adjourned," The judge announced right before he banged his gavel and exited the courtroom. A huge smile formed across my face as I reached over and wrapped my arms around Bre. Donk was escorted out of the courtroom looking like he just won the lottery. Steve walked towards me and I gave him a firm hand-shake.

"I really appreciate you for this. Call me and let me know when you get a date for Rico. Hopefully, you can do the same for him."

"Okay. For sure it would be one day this week, and you don't have to thank me this is my job. It's what I get paid to do. If you would like, you can go through my company to make his bail." Steve suggested.

"Okay, I'll follow you."

I was waiting on Donk to call while I sat across from Steve inside of his office. He got all the paperwork together to process his bond. I already had him a change of clothes in the backseat and soon as he hits the pavement, we're going to see Rochelle.

"Look, Mun, first thing in the morning I'm going to set things up to get Rico a court date." Steve said never looking up from the computer screen.

"Okay. I think I'll pay him a visit tomorrow. He haven't called and that's not like him.

Ring! Ring! Ring!

"Hello," I answered calmly trying to hide the excitement.

"You have a collect call from...Donk."

As I listened to the automated system, I contemplated whether or not I should go visit Rico today or tomorrow.

"Bro." Donk called out.

"What's up, nigga? You good?"

"Yea I'm chilling. When they gon' let me up out this bitch?"

"Steve said as soon as he processes it, I can come pick you up."

"Okay, bet. I love you, bro."

"I love you too, fam."

Click!

"Okay Mun, I'll be done in about five minutes. You can go ahead and head out, and it'll be complete by the time you make it there." Steve assured.

"I'll catch up with you tomorrow. Thanks again, man." I said, rushing out of the office. I walked out of the office feeling like a million bucks. Bre was in the passenger seat knocked out. I hopped in the whip, slamming the door purposely. She jumped up with a frightened look on her face, but when she locked eyes with me she eased back down in her seat.

"Yo' scary ass. Don't nobody want you but me." I joked.

"Yeah, whatever nigga. Where we going now?"

"To go get Donk."

I brought the engine alive and pulled out of the empty lot. It's been three days since I saw Rochelle. She took the funeral pretty hard. I hope she's better now. Maybe we'll all go out and have drinks or something. Her and Rhonda were probably getting drunk right now as I speak.

I pulled alongside of the curb in front of Dallas County Jail. I spotted Donk waiting by the bus stop with a small bag in his hand. Before I got the chance to honk the horn, he began sprinting towards the car. After witnessing an asleep Bre, he climbed into the backseat.

"Nigga, what's up?" He yelled wrapping his arms around me from behind.

"Have you heard from Rico? Is he on his way out too?"

"Nah, Steve is working on his court date. I still haven't heard from him but he'll be getting released as soon as he go to court.

"So, where we headed?"

"You can change into them clothes back there or wait to we get to mama house to change, but she been wanting to see us. I'm thinking about us all going out to eat or something."

"Hell yeah, bet. I miss her too man. I was scared as hell. I thought I wasn't going to get out."

"Well, you out. I hope you done had a change of heart 'bout certain shit. Call momma and tell her we on our way." I said hoping to talk some sense into Donk. I picked up my joint from the ashtray and fired it up.

"Aye, she didn't answer," Donk said.

"Call Rhonda's phone. She probably can't hear over that loud ass music. Rhonda was like an aunt to us. Since we were kids, she have always been around.

"What!" Donk yelled to the person on the other side of the phone. I turned around to face Donk.

"Wassup?" I asked dumbfounded to the reason for Donk's outburst.

"Where y'all at?" We on our way!" Donk yells again before hanging up the phone.

"FFFUUUUUCCCKKKKKKK!" Donk yells at the top of his lung hitting the backseat repeatedly, alerting Bre.

"Nigga wassup!" Mun ask puzzled and frustrated.

"Turn around, nigga, momma at Baylor Hospital."

Ah'Million

CHAPTER 31
RICO

I swallowed the huge lump in my throat as I watched the detectives walk back and forth. It had been nearly three days and I hadn't spoken to anyone but these bullshit ass cops. I smelled like must and shit. My stomach was touching my heart and the shit was hurting my feelings. They hadn't offered me a cup of water, let alone a bite to eat. I wonder if Donk was going through the same thing. If only we would've left when he told me to but noooo, I had to be greedy. I remember bussing at those funky ass Jamaicans, but I know for a fact I didn't kill one. Shit, if it wasn't for Donk they would've killed my ass. A few minutes later, the door from the dark holding cell opened. Two detectives walked in carrying a manila envelope. A loud thud echoed throughout the small room when the envelope hit the floor.

"Now I want you to open that envelope."

What I saw instantly made my heart drop to my toes.

CHAPTER 32
DONK

Me, Mun and Bre sprinted through the doors of Baylor Hospital. Several people occupied the lobby as we made our way to the front desk. The stench of baby shit flooded my nostrils with each stride.

"Can you tell me the room that Rochelle Richards is in?" Mun asked the oversized desk clerk. Her hair was short and thin and her eyeliner was slightly smeared. She reached underneath the desk and retrieved a large white binder. I was so anxious that I couldn't stop pacing back and forth.

"She's in room 58." She quickly informed while smacking on her chewing gum. I flew down the hallway, moving as fast as my legs would allow. As I got closer, fear kicked in and I paused before opening the door to her room. I slowly entered the room and instantly met Rochelle with tear in my eyes. Full of disappointment and dread, I looked down at her fragile body and the oxygen mask that was placed over her face.

"Rhonda brought me up here earlier." She spoke softly. Rhonda sat in the chair behind me. She looked tired as hell and her eyes were swollen like she had been crying hard and long.

"Baby, I got Sickle-Cell Anemia," she blurted out.

"What?" Mun asked.

"What is Sickle Cell?" I asked. I couldn't stand to look at her. Her legs looked as if they were crooked and her hand were bent at the fingertips. I just couldn't fucking understand.

"It's a blood disease."

I dropped my head and let the tears fall cause I knew anything of that nature was serious. I just couldn't believe the trials me and my family were enduring. I wanted to look up to the heavens and cry my soul out so God could hear me and stop all of this madness. I decided against it because with all the wrong I've done and lives I took; I knew this wasn't nothing but Karma.

My momma? Why not me? I thought.

"Ma, why didn't you tell us?" Mun asked with a timid look in his eyes.

"I was trying to find the right time to tell y'all."

But it wasn't even her fault because I do remember on several occasions, her trying to get us all under the same roof. Especially after Quaylo passed.

"So momma, you dying?" Mun asked in panic as his grip on the railing around the bed tightened. Rochelle tilted her head back to prevent the tears from falling. I could look at her and tell she was hurting. Not so much from the pain of her illness, but the pain she was causing us. It was hurting her to see us hurt. I would've never thought in a million years I would see my mother suffering at such a young age. I began to slowly shake my head as I lightly chuckled thinking about her smile. Her skin was still so smooth and radiant, and her smile was simply beautiful.

I can't believe I'm 'bout to lose my momma, I thought.

"Boys, we all have to go someday." Rochelle mumbled as she winced in pain.

"Mamma, please just hold on. It has to be a way out of this. We just lost Quay. Not you, not now. Is it a cure? How much you need? Do you need a transplant? I'll give you any organ on my body, even my heart. You brought me into this world, you can have my life." Mun spoke through tears as he bit down on his bottom lip. Not being able to control it anymore, the tears uncontrollably fell from Rochelle eyes. She reached up and placed her small hand on Mun's face. I couldn't help but to wonder how she felt. I wrapped my arms around her and said. "Momma, I know you're not in control of what is taking place, and if it was up to you, you wouldn't be in this situation. I hate the unfairness of life. I hate all this shit but just know I'm going to still remain here until they kick me out. If they think they just gone make me leave while you still have breath in your body, I'm gon' shoot my way out this bitch." I spoke through clenched teeth as my teardrops soaked her pillow.

"Excuse me, can I have ten minutes alone with Ms. Richards? The lanky doctor asked peeking his head inside of the room.

"Why can't you say it in front of all of us?" We all spoke in unison.

"Okay, well let me speak with here first. Then I'll speak with you all." He replied.

"Hell nah, nigga just tell us now It ain't no secrets. This my momma!" I yelled becoming frustrated with the peon ass doctor.

"Dontrail." Rochelle called out giving me the side eye. The doctor looked at Rochelle as if he were getting her approval. Then, he began to speak.

"Sickle cell is a very serious, yet common disease, but it isn't as deadly as it appears. You can still live a long and healthy life. However, Rochelle has a weak immune system and the disease is taking her pretty fast. She doesn't have long."

"Is it anything we can do to prevent it, or help?" Rhonda begged.

"I'm afraid not, ma'am." He responded as me, Rhonda, Mun, and Bre dropped our heads in defeat. I reached over the bed and quickly wrapped my arms around Rochelle's small frame and cried my eyes out. The doctor turned to leave.

"It's gone be okay. Y'all stop moping." Rochelle whispered with a half-smile, which instantly made my heart smile. At that moment, I realized I wasn't going to be able to stomach this shit. I could hear her small voice. But I couldn't, nor did I try to make out why she was smiling. It was nothing she could say to change the way I felt. Since I could remember, I've always been family oriented. My trust issues made me become an isolated person. My friends were my brother and sister, other than the few associates I socialized with for beneficial purposes. However, I was the true meaning of anti-social. My family was small and we were all close. It was killing me to have witness all of this tragedy.

"Donk, let me have a little time with mama." Mun announced. I slowly raised my head and kissed Rochelle on the forehead before stepping aside. I still could not believe what was actually happening. I felt so distraught, I thought I would die at this very moment from a broken heart.

Ah'Million

CHAPTER 33
MUN

Me and Donk sat in my Magnum in pure silence as I watched the raindrops slowly descend down the window.

Lil Boosie's Going Through Some Thangs played softly, only making the atmosphere increasingly gloomy. I dropped Rhonda off a few minutes ago, then parked in my mother's driveway a few doors down.

A few hours after the doctor gave us the update, she passed away. Dead or alive, I did not want to leave her side. Before she passed, she begged Donk to stay out of trouble as she quoted a scripture from the bible. "The strongest warrior doesn't always win the battle." I don't know if Donk understood, but I did.

"One thing that doesn't stop for no one is time, and I hate I wasted so much of it behind bars. I'm always locked up when the people I care about most really need me." Donk stated.

"I do six years, come home and not even two weeks later, Quay dies. Then, mama dies the day after I get released from the county. Those could've been days I could've spent with her. She was living on borrowed time and we didn't even know it. Do you think Quaylo knew?" Donk asked seemingly confused.

"I don't know. Shit, now we'll never know." When it rains, it pours but pours was such a small, yet common phrase. Shit was real and it was beyond average, for us anyway.

"So, what we going to do about mama house? I asked Donk who seemed unusually calm. I knew he was going to spazz out any minute now.

"I'll take care of the payments, but until I get the strength to live in there without breaking down every second, I'm gon' just crash at a room."

"A room? Nigga, you tripping. I got three cribs."

"Nah Mun, it ain't that. I really just don't know what I will and won't do at this point so I'm gon' just mob alone for some time so I won't put you in jeopardy." I could see the deranged look in his eyes.

"Look bruh, I love you from my soul to my toes, but this ain't no one fault. Momma died from a deadly disease, not from the hands of a human being. You can't go around shooting shit up."

"I understand, but I'm going through it."

"I know the shit easier said than done, but you got to at least try to stay sane. Do you remember what momma said before she died?"

"The strongest warrior doesn't always win the battle." Donk recited.

"In so many words, it basically means that the fastest runner doesn't always win the race. Life is full of surprises, and when you make plans it doesn't always happen the way you plan it. Every road isn't smooth. It's gone be a few bumps and potholes along the way." I preached, determined to convince Donk. Before Donk could respond, my cellphone rang.

"What's up, Steve?" I answered trying to hide the distress before putting him on speaker phone.

"Hey Mun, I got some information on your boy, but it's not good."

"Come on just tell me, Steve." Not even surprised by the fact more bullshit was coming my way

"Rico was found dead in his cell a few hours ago."

"What!" Me and Donk yelled in unison as we quickly turned and looked at each other,

"Yeah he… uh…committed suicide."

"What the fuck?"

I couldn't believe what I was hearing.

"Look, I have his property. Meet me up here at the jail so you can pick it up. You're the only person listed on his emergency contacts. You and a Rochelle Richards. I'm assuming that's his mother. I made several attempts to reach out to her but I couldn't get through."

"Rochelle is my mother and she just passed, but I'll be there shortly." I mumbled in pure disdain as I disconnected the call.

"Mun, what the fuck is going on? This some final destination shit!"

134

Nah, it probably was them pussy ass detectives. They must have scared him with their lies and he went into his cell and started tripping. That shit he was snorting didn't make it no better.

I pull up at the county jail and I spot Steve parked across the street at the gas station. Me and Donk hop out and walk towards his direction, while Steve met us halfway.

"So, how was he when they found him?" I asked Steve as we approached one another.

"Hanging from the light in his cell. He used his sheet."

"Why the fuck would he do something like that?" I asked myself out loud.

"Perhaps, he knew he was going to be locked up for a long time."

"Why is that? He know he didn't kill nobody. I got rid of the murder weapon." Donk cut in.

"Yeah, but I just found out that the gun he was brought into custody with matched the cartridge casing found at the scene where a Shaquavia Richards was shot and killed."

Ah'Million

CHAPTER 34
BRE

Today was just like any other day at Head Start. I always enjoyed coming to work. Since I was young I've had a passion for children. I probably would've been a pediatrician if I wasn't afraid of hospitals. I decided to just go the teacher route. The day was almost over and I really did miss Mun. He told me he needed a little time alone to grieve and digest everything that has happened. It's crazy how his life has changed so drastically in just a few weeks. It's been so hard being away from him, but I have to respect his wishes.

"Excuse me, Ms. Bridges, can I speak with you?" Ms. Hodges asked as she peeked inside of the classroom. Ms. Hodges was an older teacher who taught students between the ages of 3 and 6.

"Yes?"

"I have a four-year-old student who just got into an altercation with one of the other students. Can you please just keep an eye on her for me today?"

"Sure, where is she?" I asked looking over Ms. Hodges shoulders. Ms. Hodges stepped to the side and behind her stood the timid looking girl. Her clothes were torn and dingy, yet she had some of the most alluring features, despite her hair being all over her head.

"Come on in, sweetie. What is your name?" I asked grabbing a hold of her small hand. She looked up at me then looked back down at the floor. I knelt down in front of her.

"Look, you don't have to be afraid, just relax. You can hang out with me in here for the rest of the day." I assured.

"Okay," she responded lifting her head up."

"Now, tell me your name."

"Kadejah," she whispered.

"Class, this is Kadejah. She will be joining us today." I announced.

"Hello, Kadejah!" The students yelled in unison. Kadejah seemed to loosen up a bit.

"Go ahead and find you a group." I said. I watched her mingle with the other kids before I diverted my attention to the messy pile of paperwork that covered my desk.

"Guys, do not forget tomorrow is show and tell." I announced.

"Okay, Ms. Bridges." A few responded. It was the beginning of the school year and show and tell has always been a great way for me to personally get to know the children better.

"Ms. Bridges?" Kadejah called out. I turned around giving her my undivided attention.

"Yes, sweetie?"

"Can I please stay in your class? I don't want to go back to Ms. Hodges class. The kids are mean to me over there." Kadejah confided.

"Mean? How?" I asked curiously folding my arms across my chest.

"Ummmm…" She looked down at her feet and said. "They talk about me. They say bad stuff about my shoes and clothes."

When I looked down at Kadejah's shoes, I noticed her big toe peeking out the side of her left shoe, while she continuously wiggled her toes to hide it. I instantly felt sorrowful for the little girl, but *one who struggles, has the most ambition*, I thought. I looked into her eyes, so I wouldn't continue to make her feel uncomfortable.

"I will talk to Ms. Hodges to see if we can transfer you over to my class permanently. Kadejah smiled. "Okay." She had a beautiful smile.

"Okay class, put you're folders up so you can be dismissed." I announced. All the students scrambled to put their things away. I opened the door and stepped into the hallway. I peeped inside of Ms. Hodges class across the way to get her attention.

"Yes, Ms. Bridges?" She asked walking towards the door.

"I wanted to know if you would be okay with transferring Kadejah to my class." She paused for a minute, as if the question surprised her.

"Are you sure?" She's a handful."

"I'm positive." I responded.

138

"Okay, I'll take her name off my roster and I'll have her folder ready for you first thing in the morning." She assured with a huge grin on her face. She seemed more excited than Kadejah about the swap. I stepped back into the classroom to make sure everything was put away.

"Kadejah," I called out squatting down in front of her.

"Yes ma'am?"

"I'm your new teacher." I smiled anticipating her reaction.

"Yes! She yelled wrapping her arms around my neck. I was taken aback by her affection. She was so precious.

"I'm excited as well, sweetie." I said with a slight chuckle as I stood to my feet and walked to my desk. Minutes passed, and one by one the student were being picked up by their parents. I couldn't wait to get off and call to check on Mun. I hate the fact we couldn't get through his troubles together. Suddenly, I was down to two students. Martin and Kadejah. Martin's parents were usually twenty minutes late.

"Kadejah, who picks you up?" I asked.

"My mom," she said, looking around nervously.

"Is she usually late?"

"Sometimes, because she picks up my brothers and sisters."

"How many siblings do you have?"

"Huh?" Kadejah asked confused with my choice of words. I chuckled.

"How many sisters and brothers do you have?"

"Twelve"

My eyes widened instantly and I was taken back once again.

"Ms. Bridges?" Ms. Hodges called out with her briefcase in her hand as she stood by the door.

"Yes?" I responded walking toward her.

"Sometimes Kadejah's mom doesn't show because it's so many of them to tend to. So after about thirty minutes, I usually take it upon myself to drop her off." Ms. Hodges advised.

"How far away does she live from here?"

"Oh, not far at all. She stays in the orphanage right down the street."

"The orphanage?" I asked as the wrinkles formed across my forehead.

"Yes Ms. Bridges, Kadejah is an orphan." I looked over at Kadejah who was looking out the window with her face buried inside of her palms.

"Okay, I'll see you tomorrow," she said before walking down the hall.

"Come on, Kadejah. I'm going to take you home," I said as I grabbed my keys and Versace purse off the desk.

"Okay, Ms. Bridges!" Kadejah screamed as she ran from the window with a huge grin on her face.

As me and Kadejah exited the school building, I couldn't help but think about her situation. No wonder she was so poorly dressed. Most foster parents don't give a damn about the children. They just want the money.

"Which one is yours Ms. Bridges?" Kadejah yelled as she ran through the parking lot.

"That one right here, the white one." I said pointing towards my white 2015 Range Rover.

"It's pretty. I want one like this when I get big." Kadejah said in amazement. I chuckled to myself while unlocking the door. This little girl was amusing. I checked my phone for any missed calls or text hoping to see Mun's name, but there wasn't anything. I missed him so much and hated the separation shit.

"Ms. Bridges, can you turn that up?" Kadejah asked bobbing her head.

"Girl, what you know about that?" I chuckled as I turned up the volume to Young M.A new song, *Ooohhhh*. Kadejah sang along as I cruised through the streets. I thought about my plans, although Mun wanted his own seed. I really was considering the process of adopting a child. I'm tired of waiting around for something I know that can't happen, and now that he knows, I can speed the process along to make our family complete.

I pulled up to the house where Kadejah lived. Once I came to a stop, her grin went away as she slowly unbuckled the seat belt.

"I'll see you tomorrow, okay?" I asked trying to lift her suddenly sad spirit.

"Okay, Ms. Bridges." She responded as she opened the door and walked to her front door. Whoever opened the door for her didn't even bother to look out and see how she had gotten home. I just shook my head in disbelief and drove off once Kadejah was safely inside.

Ah'Million

CHAPTER 35
DONK

All along it was a nigga in my circle who caused me and my family all this decrement and depression. I knew the nigga was not be trusted, but I didn't know to what extent. I could've walked in the County and murked that nigga myself. I can't believe that shit happen right underneath my nose. I've always seen through the bullshit and protected Quay. I should've been took care of that nigga.

"You told me 'bout that nigga, bruh." Mun said with his head down. I could sense his frustration.

"It ain't yo' fault. I should've just killed the nigga when we found out he was stealing, and Quay would still be here." I responded looking down at the barrel of my 9mm Desert Eagle.

"I just want to know why would he kill Quay? What's his motive?" Mun asked confused.

"That's what I'm trying to figure out."

"Quay was like a sister to him."

"I still think they had some funny shit going on, but I'll find out something once I get comfortable and charge up his phone."

"You sure you don't want to come to my place? It's just me."

"Nah fam, look I'm 'bout to duck off for a few days, get me some cash, head out of town to a whole new scenery and get my mind right." I said reaching for my car keys.

"Shit, where you want to go?" Mun asked hopping off the couch,

"Before I go anywhere I'm goin' to see what family Rico has still alive."

"I told you. All he had was me, momma, and Quay."

"That's cool, but I'm gon' double check."

"I understand."

"I'll catch up with you later." I stated stuffing my keys into my pocket before walking out of the door. I hated to leave Mun with everything going on, but with the state of mind I was in, it was best he stay away from me.

I merged onto Highway 35 and called Jeff. "Aye Jeff, I need you to give me any and I mean any member of the family." I began speaking as soon as he answered.

"Okay, send me the information."

I immediately hung up the phone and sent Jeff Rico's information.

Jeff: Demunte Richards is the only person I found, but I can go deeper into my database when I get to my office in the morning.

I sat down my phone once I finished reading the text. Something in me is telling me he has someone outside of my family. I could be wrong but I'm gone know for sure before I just throw the towel in.

I called an old friend of mine named Big Ace. I give credit when it's due and Big Ace was a real standup guy. He was a known jack boy back in the day, but when his right hand man got killed, he let it all go. Now he was living the normal everyday life, playing family man and enjoying retirement. Although he didn't live that life no more, he was still plugged in. Motherfuckas would inform him on major money moves, hoping he'll pick the tool and mask up, but he never did.

"Yo wassup, Ace?"

"Damn, it's been a long time my boy. Pull up on me, I'm at the car wash on Bruton.

"Bet."

Immediately, I took the next exit and headed into the opposite direction. Without a doubt, I know he would have something lined up. My mind was just so far gone I couldn't focus. I looked over at the passenger seat where Rico's phone laid. I couldn't wait to get home so I could see what lies within.

I pull up to the car wash and parked next to Big Ace's royal blue Chrysler 300. Big Ace was seated on top of the trunk when I hopped out my whip. He looked a bit older, but he was still dressed sharp as a razor blade. We shook hands while he looked around suspiciously. He always acted so suspect like he was as guilty as the next motherfucka.

"Aye, I got something for ya." He spoke in a low tone close to a whisper.

"Rap."

"A young Italian nigga name Sunny. The boy making some noise. He moving major weight. At first, I thought the nigga was bullshittin' me until I checked shit out for myself. I watched him for a couple of days. He don't keep much muscle around him. He real flashy and he move careless and reckless."

"Where the nigga sleep at?"

"A condo in North Dallas."

I really wasn't too fond of North Dallas. It was always some shady shit going on out there and the laws never slept. Niggas acted like bitches, while the bitches acted like reptiles, snakes to be exact. So I just kept my distance, but I'm willing to step out of my comfort zone for this one.

"Oh yeah, I'm on that ASAP. Go ahead and text me the address." I replied anxiously walking back to my ride.

"Alright bet. Be easy, blood." Big Ace yelled as he held his double cup of drank towards the sky. I drove off to go stake out the scene. When I heard my phone ringing, Jeff's name flashed across the screen.

"Yeah," I said anxiously.

"Aye, I should have something for you in two days." He assured.

"Okay, call me then." I replied hanging up the phone. I was desperate for anything at this point. Ex-girlfriend, cousin, pet. I don't give a damn.

CHAPTER 36
BRE

I sat at my desk in front of the computer screen researching the requirements to adopt a child. Kadejah had been on my mind heavy since the first day I took her home, and I couldn't deny the fact that I really adored this little girl. It was something peculiar about her that made her stand out from the other kids. I really wanted to introduce her to the finer things in life. Me and Mun had money to blow, might as well give to the less fortunate. I hadn't asked Mun about it and I wasn't sure about his response to the situation.

Kadejah was just misunderstood if you ask me. She was very smart, yet curious about a lot of things, but she was still innocent and passive. She had no clue, but I was really considering making her a part of me and Mun's family. The requirements were simple. Paperwork, drug test, interview, and background check. Although Mun sold dope, we were stable in all aspects of life. Well other than the emotional stress Mun was currently enduring.

"Ms. Bridges, what are you looking at?" Kadejah asked pointing at the computer screen.

"Girl, you so nosey" I chuckled before spinning my chair around to face her.

"Ms. Bridges, can you buy me ice cream when you take me home today, pweese?" She asked rocking back and forth.

"Yes Kadejah, come here for a second." I yelled from across the room.

"Yes?" she responded politely.

"Do you know you're real mother and father?" I asked with squinted eyes.

"I have a picture of me and my mom when I was born, but I never seen my dad." She replied looking down at her small hands. "If you don't mind, can you bring the picture to school with you tomorrow?"

"Yes ma'am, Ms. Bridges."

As Kadejah made her way to her seat, I continued to absorb the information on the screen. The more I read; I became even more anxious. I couldn't wait to run my plan by Mun. I just hope he'll support my decision and agree with my choice.

Mun was finally ready for a bitch to come home, and I didn't know how to act. I hurried up and dropped Kadejah off after I grabbed her two vanilla ice cream cones from McDonalds. My plan was to take her to my favorite buffet and let her eat however much ice cream she wanted, but when I received Mun text not too long ago, I switched up the whole plan.

I went home and freshened up before heading over to Mun's condo he'd been staying in. Now, I was standing on the other side of the door waiting to see his face. When the door opened, it was as if the whole world stopped. I never felt so many emotions at one time. Despite Mun being emotionally stressed, he was still so fucking sexy. His beard was thicker than usual and his hair wasn't freshly edged up, but the rugged look he portrayed made my pussy pulsate.

"Hey daddy, I missed you," I said as I tightly wrapped my arms around his neck not wanting to let go.

"Damn you missed me, huh?" He asked stepping back taking in my beauty. I don't know what he was thinking, but I know I was ready to make up for lost time. Mun stepped to the side and I sashayed past him. My long and expensive bundles only complimented my tight fitted Versace v-cut dress that I wore. He knew I missed him; my face expression alone was enough. I looked around the elegant but empty condo. I could feel Mun's breath on my neck as he grabbed me by my waist. His touch instantly made me weak and I could feel my pussy throbbing. The way Mun made me feel was gratifying, yet unusual. I didn't know my body could react in a manner to another person's touch. I quickly slid out of my gold red bottoms and turned around until I was face to face with Mun. I don't know if it was the love I had for him, but this nigga was so sexy to me. Before he could say anything, I dropped to my knees, eased his dick out of his pants and commenced to sucking the skin off his shit. I eyed him closely while I took his monster in and out of my mouth.

"Fuck!" He yelled as he grabbed the back of my head and sexed my face until he released inside of my mouth. I swallowed every drop, then used my tongue to clean up his mess by licking and slurping his rod from the tip to the shaft.

"Give me some dick." I demanded as I stood to my feet and began stripping out of my dress. He stroked his dick while he patiently watched me undress. I slowly removed my bra and panties and before I could toss my bra to the side, he walked towards me and bent me over the couch. He pressed his erection against my pussy and without warning, he eased himself inside of me. I arched my back and stood on the tip of my toes, allowing him better access to my pussy.

"Oooooohhhhhhh Mun, this yo' pussy daddy." I moaned as I bit down on my bottom lip. I felt like I was in Heaven.

"Oh yeah? You love this dick?" He teased while long stroking my kitty from the back. He grabbed a handful of my hair, yanking my head backwards as he thrust himself deeper inside of me until he exploded.

"Damn daddy, I missed that dick." I softly spoke before collapsing on the couch. Mun walked toward me and stood over me with his still rock hard dick in his hand.

"You ready for another round?"

CHAPTER 37
DONK

I sat in the car across the lot from Sunny's condo. I turned up my bottle of Hennessey as I waited patiently for Sunny to arrive. The area was extremely nice and quiet. It was actually a part of North Dallas I never seen. An hour passed and still no sign of Sunny. I could hear my stomach growling, but I ignored it and continued to sip on the brown liquor that burned my insides with every swallow. I slowly tilted my head back and slightly turned the volume up allowing the music to temporarily invade my thoughts.

Awakening moments later in the same position only with the exception of drool seeping onto the collar of my grey Lacoste shirt, I looked down at the time on my watch and realized only thirty minutes had passed. I mentally debated whether or not I wanted to grab a bite to eat, but before I could decide, Sunny made the decision for me. I spotted the yellow and black Bentley merge into the reserved parking spot in front of his condo. Big Ace was right. His car alone screamed flashy. A few minutes pass and Sunny hops out of his Bentley with a female in tow. Shawty was gun thick. Sunny was actually a lot smaller than what I imagined. I quickly reached behind me and grabbed my all black Nike hoodie and put it on. They both seemed a bit tipsy. He was exactly what Big Ace described. He wore a black and gold Versace velour suit and at least six gold chains hung from his neck. Sunny laughed and joked around carefree, while he fumbled around in his pockets for the keys. He was laughing so hard that he never heard me walk up behind him.

"Open the motherfuckin' door." I mumbled loudly with both twin Glocks pressed against the back of both of their skulls. Sunny instantly dropped his keys and threw his hands up in the air.

"Pick them keys up and open the door and don't say shit." I demanded shoving him in the back of the head with the pistol. The female was now sweating profusely. I could tell she wanted to cry out for help, but one false movement and her brains gon' be all over the doorstep.

"What's this all about? How much you want?" Sunny asked nervously fidgeting with his keys.

"Just open the door, nigga!" I yelled becoming impatient. The sound of the door unlocking was music to my ears. Not knowing what to expect, I shoved Sunny and his female friend inside.

"Look, please don't kill me!" Sunny begged before crashing into the coffee table.

"Go get everything. The drugs, money, and artillery." I demanded aiming the gun in his direction as I grabbed the female by her hair. To my surprise, it was a wig, and it came off as quickly as I reached for it. I quickly tossed the wig to the side and for the first time I took a really good glance at shawty. I shook my head in disbelief when I noticed the masculine features that stuck out like a sore thumb.

"Fucking faggots. Go get my shit!" I yelled grabbing the punk by the top of his dress placing my pistol to his back while we trailed Sunny around the house. Sunny's crib was decked out.

Everything was neatly organized and every room I bypassed was fully furnished. We came to a stop at what seemed to be the Master bedroom. He walked over to a door and inserted a code into what resembled a closet. I had never seen so much dope in one spot. Stacks of money were piled up in one corner of the closet. The bright light inside of the walk-in closet only enhanced the quality of the bricks that were neatly stacked on the middle and upper shelf. My eyes grew wide in astonishment as he placed every brick and stack inside the duffle bags. Every so often he would look back at me with pleading eyes. When he got down to the last brick, I silenced the faggot with one bullet to the back of his skull, dropping him instantly. Sunny smiled as I walked towards him, knowing what was about to take place.

"Go ahead, kill me, but just know nothing that involves Sunny goes unseen, my boy." He stated bravely, no longer pleading for his life. I sent two bullets into his chest and fired another shot striking him in the neck, before his body collapsed onto the floor. I grabbed all three bags and made my exit. I paused once I reached the front door. I noticed the shadows bypass the window. Off impulse, I quickly ducked behind the leather sofa. Before I could check the clip in my 9mm, three armed men rushed inside the house. They were all going in different directions. I didn't know whether to stay and shoot it out or run for the door which was only a few feet away. Ignoring my first mind, I scurried from behind the couch and ran out of the already opened front door, only to be met by two more armed men who stood beside Sunny's car. Shots sprang out instantly as I ducked behind the mailbox made of bricks. I fired two shots in one of the men's direction hitting him in the throat, and the side of his head. I looked around precisely while trying to find a way out, knowing the three men inside will soon be on my ass as well. Shots rang out from a distance that startled me. I looked past the mailbox to see Big Ace shooting multiple bullets into the other dudes direction, dropping him instantly.

"Nigga go! I got you. Go Now! Hurry up!" He yelled with his pistol hanging out of his window. I darted towards my car, only to hear more shots being fired into my direction. I turned around to fire back and saw two of the three armed men chasing me.

"Aaarrgggghhhhhh." I roared out as a bullet pierced my left shoulder. I regretted parking so far away. Another one of the men yelped out in pain before hitting the concrete. Big Ace continued to fire at the men. Ignoring the burning, yet painful sensation in my shoulder, I looked behind me and opened fire, hitting the last dude in the leg. He still fired his gun into my direction while he lay on the ground. Big Ace drove alongside of the gunman, striking him two times in the head putting him out of his misery. Finally reaching my car, I hopped in not wanting to waste any more time fleeing the scene.

I pulled up to Rochelle's house with Big Ace in tow.

"You good?" I replied opening my car door.

"How did you know to come?" I asked curiously, looking at the man who saved my life.

"About an hour ago, my little informant laced me up on Sunny's muscle and why they weren't never with him and that when I found out his car and house is under surveillance They can watch him from a distance on they're phones."

"Word?" I asked in amazement.

"I was just gon' call you and warn you, but I said fuck it. I wouldn't be able to live with myself, if something would've happened to you and I wasn't there to help. I'm the one told you about the mission." I eased out of my car and pulled Big Ace into a tight hug.

"I preciate ya fam, for real. I owe you one. I'm gon' drop you off something tomorrow."

"Nah nigga, I didn't do that for no favor. You don't owe me shit. Real niggas do real shit. All I want you to do, if you can at least consider the idea of getting out of the game young blood. You see how close you was to death? Use that dope to take off and you'll be set. I'm telling you what I know and what I did."

First Mun, then Rochelle and now Big Ace was telling me the same thing. The only difference between me and Big Ace was…I didn't have nothing to live for.

"Alright, fam." I said before Big Ace took off towards his car. I grabbed the bags out of the backseat, and carefully placed one on top of my injured shoulder.

Once inside, I emptied the bags and counted everything and separated the bricks from the money. The bullet wound was starting to make my eye lids feel heavy.

In the midst of putting everything back into the bags, the sound of my phone ringing startled me. I reach into pocket and sees its Persuasia calling.

"Hello?" I answer nonchalantly into the phone.

"Can I get some time?"

I hesitated before responding, but then I realized maybe this is a perfect time. I am in need of a nurse.

"Yeah, come fuck with me."

"Okay, text me the address. I'm on my way."

With that being said, I hung the phone and immediately texted Persuasia the address. I was so caught up on the lick that I didn't realize I was standing in an empty house. I could see my momma in the kitchen right now fixing me a hot plate. I missed her so much that words can't explain. A tear fell from my eye when I thought about her smile. I wiped my face and put everything into the closet so that I could get myself together before Persuasia arrives.

A few minutes later, I hear a knock at the door. I grab my strap off the table as I walk toward the door. A smile forms across my face when I see Persuasia standing in front of me looking like a piece of steak. Her nude dress only covered so much of her enticing body.

"Damn girl, hurry up and get in here." I teased.

"You so funny, boy." She chuckled walking past me.

"What the hell happened to your shoulder? She asked stepping into my personal space.

"I got shot a few minutes ago. Can you take a look at it for me?" I asked. She was so close I could feel her breathe. Her lips were so juicy and succulent. It was hard for me to control myself.

"Sit down, you should've been said something." She stated as she ran past me and into the kitchen. She retrieved a small bowl of water and a few utensils. I didn't bother to see what all she had, I just let her go to work.

"You know what you doing?" I asked sarcastically sitting in the chair at the dining room table.

"Of course, I've done this same procedure hundreds of times with my older brothers." She assured pouring the water over the wound.

"Shit! That hurt!" I yelped out in pain as the sharp object dug into my skin.

"Well, it looks like the bullet just grazed you. It took a piece of your flesh with it but at least it didn't go in." She stated dropping the steak knife onto the table.

"Do you have any bandages?"

"Yeah, they in the lower cabinet in the restroom, Dr. P" I joked watching Persuasia's ass switch from side to side as she bypassed me.

She returns seconds later and cleans up the wound before placing the bandage over it.

"Can we finish what we started?" I asked as I wrapped my arms around her tiny waist while she stood in between my legs massaging my temples with her hands.

"I would love to." She stated taking a few steps back allowing me space to get up. I walked over to the bar and grabbed the half full bottle of Hennessey, followed by two shot glasses.

"Can you handle this or do you prefer something clear?" I teased knowing she probably preferred something a bit fruity.

"Oh, I can handle that." She shot back.

"We'll see." I smirked. After two shots, Persuasia was kicking off her Jimmy Choo's and peeling off her dress. I sat there and watched her as she begin to get comfortable. She stood there wearing nothing but a pink lace bra and matching boy shorts. I could no longer contain myself. I started stripping out of my Nike sweatpants and Polo boxer briefs. I tossed them to the side with nothing left but an empty shot glass that I held in my left hand. I put it on the table before sitting on the loveseat. Persuasia followed my lead and stripped out of her bra and panties, revealing her pretty nicely shaved pink pussy.

"Bring your sexy ass over here," I said while I stroked my dick with one hand.

"You sure you want this?" She teased as she leaned forward and placed my mans in her mouth. She sucked on it nice and slow, letting saliva drip all over the place. I moaned and groaned while I grabbed her head in ecstasy.

"OH shit, Fuck!" I groaned loudly slowly thrusting myself into her wet mouth.

"I'm about to nut." I mumbled as my eyes began to roll to the back of my head.

I quickly picked her up and carried her into the kitchen. Once I placed her ass onto the countertop, I placed soft wet kisses onto her lips. I kissed her while rubbing my dick up and down her pussy before entering her wet cave. Once I broke through her barrier, she gasped for air. I slowed my pace, gripping her ass cheeks as she moaned and spreaded Persuasia's legs wider. With every stroke, her moans grew louder and louder which only aroused me even more. Her pussy was wet and tight. After a few strokes, I began to pound harder losing the little control I had left. Feeling her freshly manicured nails in my back only made me tighten my grip. Persuasia wrapped her legs around my waist ceasing my long strokes. I deeply plunged in and out of her pussy, nearly touching her stomach. Her walls became snug and tight and I could tell she was about to bust.

"Don't stop bae, fuck me nigga!" She cried out, breathing heavily as she wrapped her arms weakly around my neck. I also released pulling her into my chest and carrying her to the bedroom.

"Damn nigga, I didn't know you put it down like that," she said running her hand through my fade as we lay face to face.

"It's a lot you don't know." I shot back, watching her slowly drift off.

I awoke to my phone ringing and it was messages from Jeff and Persuasia. From the looks of it, she left while I was asleep with my phone in my right hand. I walked around the house to assure nothing was missing or out of order. I checked the closet first and everything seemed to be in place.

Persuasia: I enjoyed myself last night and I hope we can link up again soon.

I smirked while reading the text message as I replayed events from last night.

Jeff: Call me ASAP.

Jeff: Call me

Jeff: I got someone

After seeing the multiple messages from Jeff, I quickly dialed his number.

"It's a kid, Donk." He informed as soon as he picked up the phone.

"That's all you have?" I asked somewhat sympathetic.

"Yes, that's all I have. Other than her, he has no more relatives."

"Okay, fuck it. It is what it is. Go ahead and text me the address and a brief description of the kid."

"Okay."

I hung up the phone and grabbed my car keys off the table. Kid or not. I don't discriminate. The nigga didn't hesitate to pop my sister. As soon as I hopped in the whip, Jeff sent me all the information that I would need to pinpoint the child, and now I was ready and headed that way.

CHAPTER 38
BRE

Bright and early Tuesday morning, all of the kids came pouring into the classroom. I was in a wonderful mood. I finally was back home with Mun and I was able to muster up enough courage to ask Mun about Kadejah and to my surprise he thought it was a great idea. I couldn't wait to tell her; I know she's going to be ecstatic. Even though I hadn't spoken to my mom about every-thing, I decided to pay her a visit today once I leave work.

"Hey, Ms. Bridges!" Kadejah yelled running towards me wrapping her arms around my neck.

"Hey, you okay?" I chuckled at her level of affection.

"Yes ma'am U, excuse me, Ms. Bridges" Kadejah said as she bent down and retrieved the picture from her sock, handing it to me before running out of the door. I looked at the picture and immediately noticed the woman in the hospital bed that held Kadejah's small body. I could not believe my eyes as my mouth fell open in awe.

"Khadejah!" I yelled after her, but she was already out of the door.

"Ms. Hodges, keep an eye on my class for a second." I stated while she looked at me confused. I quickly darted past her to catch up with Kadejah.

Once I reached the front desk, I looked around in panic when I didn't see Kadejah nowhere in sight.

"Excuse me, where is the little girl that was just up here?" I asked terrified and out of breath.

"Her uncle just came and picked her up early." She responded.

"Her uncle?" I asked confused. Knowing that Kadejah is a foster child. I rushed to the front entrance catching nothing but the tail of the vehicle. I pulled out my phone and dialed Mun's number.

He picked up on the first ring.

"Come to my job…now! It's an emergency."

Ah'Million

CHAPTER 39
MUN

As I stared at the picture Bre just handed me, tears came to my eyes and I couldn't believe what I was seeing. I thought long and strong trying to understand how something so bizarre happened right underneath my nose. *How the fuck did I not notice something like that? Why did Quaylo keep it a secret and disown her seed?* I thought.

"Look I'm about to link up with Donk and we gon' put our eyes and ears to the streets and find Kadejah. I promise I'm not coming home without her. You just make sure the paper is finalized cause she's not going back to that foster home."

"Okay." Bre responded with tears in her eyes as I planted a kiss on her cheek before walking out of the school leaving her standing in the middle of the hallway.

I began to dial Donk's number when I received an incoming call from Lito.

"Waddup boi!" I spoke rapidly into the phone.

"Mun. I remember where I know your little brother from. He robbed me years ago when I was just a runner working at one of my uncle's spots." He teased slowly but seriously.

"That shit old. Come on Lito, he's hot headed." I tried desperately to convince, not having time for another altercation.

"Mun, that's not why I'm calling you."

"Then, what's up? Rap Lito."

"Someone robbed and killed my nephew last night and it's your brother. I have him on tape. He got me once, and now a second time, but I guarantee you it won't be a third. So be ready. I'm coming and you know how I'm coming." Lito said before hanging up the phone.

At first, I paused slowly taking it all in. I know how Lito rock. *He been a don in these streets for years. My team is no match for his. Were extremely outnumbered. Fuck it, we gon' be hell when they come for us*, I thought as I hopped in my ride and sped off.

CHAPTER 40
DONK

I looked down at my screen and seen Mun's name and picture.

"Aye, nig—"

"Bro, did you know Rico had a little girl?" I asked cutting him off.

"What?"

"Yeah, Jeff sent me the info a couple minutes ago and I just left from snatching the rug rat.

"Wait. Hold up. You got a little girl with you?" Mun asked in bewilderment as I sped through the light.

"Yeah nigga, Rico little girl."

"You got her form the Headstart on Lake June?"

"Yeah, how you know? I asked as the wrinkles formed on my forehead while looking down at the phone.

"Nigga that little girl is Quaylo's daughter! I'm holding a picture of her holding her at the hospital after she gave birth. Bre was gon' adopt her today, but she came up missing from the school right after Kadejah handed her the picture."

"What?" I asked in disbelief as I eyed the little girl.

"So wait, this Rico and Quaylo baby?" I asked with a wide eyed, yet unbelieving expression almost dropping my phone.

"Yeah, the picture is solid proof. I'm for sure it's Quay's and Jeff told you it was Rico's"

I looked over at the little girl again who sat calmly in the passenger seat and after staring at her closely for the first time, she did favor Quaylo. To be honest, she resembled Rochelle as well.

"Okay, now that's understood. You need to be on your toes and meet me at the spot ASAP!"

"For what? It's an Amber Alert out for her or something?"

"Nah. That lick you just hit. He was Lito's nephew and he coming for us. He got you on tape."

"He what—"

My words were cut short when I looked down and noticed the red beam on baby girl's chest. But before I could react, it was too late…

CHAPTER 41
MUN

I arrive to the scene and see Donk's CTS in the middle of the intersection. I quickly unbuckled my seatbelt and ran to his aid, only to find his body riddled with bullets. He was slumped on top of little Kadejah's body. My heart dropped and knees buckled at the overwhelming sight. I pulled Donk out of the driver seat and onto the pavement when Kadejah looked up at me with tears in her eyes. I instantly checked Donk who was coughing instantly. A faint smile spread across his face and I noticed the blood that stained his teeth.

"Come on nigga. Stay in there, you strong. You built for shit like this. Fight! Fight!" I yelled shaking him outrageously. I could hear the sirens getting closer. I sat on the pavement covered in blood while drool fell from my lips and tears fell from my eyes, as I rocked Donk back and forth until the paramedics arrived. I really needed him to make it through this.

Not even two minutes pass and the paramedics arrive at the scene and immediately rush towards us. I moved out of the way while one of them checked Donk for a pulse.

"He's not breathing, but he has a faint pulse!" He called out. I help lift his body onto the gurney as they loaded him onto the truck.

"Sir, are you a relative?" The officer asks.

"That's my brother." I responded as I lifted one leg onto the truck suddenly realizing Kadejah was in my car.

"Go without me, I'm going to follow y'all in my own ride." I yelled out while I ran back to my car. Kadejah was sitting in the passenger seat with her knees to her chest. She looked so frightened. She had been through and witnessed so much in just one day...

"It's gon' be okay, Lil Quay. Just relax." I assured while I put the car in drive and sped off behind the ambulance truck.

"Um.... My name is Kadejah," she said staring into my direction with her big bedroom eyes. I smirked at her comment.

"I know it's Kadejah, but it's a long story. I'll tell you all about it over a bowl of ice cream once this is all taken care of."

"Ooooohhhh, I love ice cream. I just looove ice cream." She chanted. I couldn't help but to smile. She possessed such an angelic charm and every time I looked at her I saw Quaylo. I reached into my pocket and shot bae a text.

Me: Meet me at Methodist Hospital ASAP

Bre: omw

I slid the phone into my jeans saying a silent prayer for Donk. He was all I had left.

Me and Kadejah sat in the lobby waiting for the nurse to give me permission to see Donk. He had been shot six times and shit was looking iffy. Kadejah was fast asleep on my chest when Bre came rushing through the hospital doors. She instantly spotted me and Kadejah in the lobby.

"What happened, Mun. Is everything alright? She asked in an alarmed tone. Even with no makeup on, she was still so beautiful. Her long Brazilian bundles fell freely down her back, her eyebrows were perfectly arched and even though she sported just a PINK sweat suit, it revealed her flat stomach and fastidious curves.

"Look, it's a long story, Donk is in ICU fighting for his life. All I need you to do is take Kadejah home and I'll call you when I know something." I promised.

"Okay, I love you." She responded before walking out of the door. I slouched down in my seat as I began to flash on the past.

(Past Event)

"Look, when the door opens, we gon' slide in," Mun whispered to Donk as they squatted down on side of the porch. Soon as the junkie emerged from the spot, in unison, they lifted their guns and rushed inside.

"Get down or lay down!" Mun yelled while Donk ran into a different direction collecting the drugs and money that sat on top of the kitchen counter.

"Please don't kill me. Y'all can have everything." The dude pleaded laying on his stomach. He seemed to be the only one in the spot. Mun darted across the room where he spotted an AR-15 and a 12 gauge pump positioned on top of a table that sat in the corner of the room. He swiftly picked them up, placing both guns in the duffel bag.

"Please man, I swear I won't say shit to nobody. Just don't kill me." The dude repeated as he lay on the floor. Donk continued to ramble through the kitchen while Mun slowly walked over to the dude and kicked him in his side causing him to clutch his side as he yelled out in pain.

"Shut the fuck up and give me that grill out yo' mouth.' Mun said through clenched teeth as he pried the dude's mouth open with his thumb and index finger snatching the gold grill out of his mouth.

"Aye Donk, come check this nigga pockets before we go!" Donk bent the corner and quickly rushed over to search the dude pockets. He pulled out a wad of money and stuffed it into his back pocket before kicking the man in the face.

"Come on fam, let's go." Mun stated zipping up the duffel bag.

"Right now?" Donk asked sarcastically meeting my gaze with a menacing stare like something possessed him.

"Yeah, right now nigga. Come on before them other dudes come back!" Mun pleaded. Donk continue to walk slowly in circles around the dude who lay on the floor.

"Go on without me, I'm right behind you." Donk assured.

"Nigga, I ain't leaving you, What the fuck you waiting on Donk? Let's go!" Mun yelled irritated. Without responding, Donk followed Mun to the front door, but stopped in mid stride firing six shots into the man's body before running behind Mun. The shit scared the shit out of Mun. Taking a life wasn't part of the plan, only if necessary, but Mun figured Donk was up to no good by the way he looked at him. Quaylo peeked her head out the window of her car when she saw them running out the house.

"Come on y'all, its helicopters lurking and shit!" She yelled pointing upwards to the helicopters that flew right above the street. She sped off into the night once Mun and Donk were safely inside the car. A feeling of relief came over Mun. He looked over at Donk who was staring a hole in his head. The raggedy ass motor in Quaylo's Buick Lumina made it hard to hear but in a low tone and a scrunched face a bit confused Mun asked Donk.

"Why did you pop ol' boy?"

"Between me and you and its cool to tell big sis if she ask, but bro you slipped up when you said my name and once an identity is revealed all witnesses got to go. Once he finds you, he will find me. I don't need us looking over our shoulders everywhere we go and if something happen to you, I'll go loco."

"You right." Mun responded shaking his head in approval meeting Donks gaze. However, the whole time he was thinking to himself that he couldn't believe his younger brother had just caught a body.

Since the age of thirteen from that day and the days ahead, I knew Donk meant business. Til this day, nothing ever came to surface about dude we left for dead. I never met another nigga as zero tolerant and stiff as Donk. Since a youngin he was solid and on everything I know love and respect, I'm goin' get that nigga Lito.

CHAPTER 42
(ONE YEAR LATER)
BRE

Me and Kadejah sat in the back of the courtroom, while Mun and his lawyer stood in front of the judge. The day Donk was shot Mun went to the hospital to support him and the detectives were waiting outside of Donk's room to identify the owner of the CTS. Unknowingly, Donk had two kilos of cocaine in the backseat of his car when everything went down. When the detectives questioned Mun, he immediately claimed the kilos, not wanting Donk to go back to prison. Mun never even spent a night in jail. He figured his chances of getting out were higher than Donk's. That day Mun was cuffed and escorted to the county jail and today he's still locked up. Being behind those walls with everything that has happened, you could look at him and tell it has taken a toll on him. When I look into his eyes, I don't even see the same Mun; nothing bothers him and his eyes are cold without a hint of emotion. Through all he's been through, I would've died a long time ago. Steve informed me it was an eight percent chance Mun would be released today, but with minor stipulations. Kadejah sat next to me playing a video game on the iPad I purchased her for her fifth birthday. She wore her hair in a ponytail exposing her curly baby hairs, with a dark purple and lime green Puma warmup suit with matching sneakers. She sported a 14-carat gold necklace with a "Lil Quay" medallion attached to it. It was a birthday gift as well from Donk. Over the months, I've really grown attached to Kadejah, and I'm so glad Ms. Hodges brought her to my class that day.

"Ma, you crying?" Kadejah asked holding my hand.

"No baby. I'm okay, just finish playing your game." I responded.

I listened intently to the D.A. lie and paint a picture to the judge as if Mun was just a menace to society.

"Fucking saltine" I mumbled.

"Ma, what you say?" She looked at me quizzically. I slightly chuckled and put my index finger to my lips to silence her.

"Yes, your honor my defendant did have two kilos of cocaine in his possession, but he never even had a traffic ticket." Steve announced to the judge.

"I object, your honor. It's true Mr. Richards never caught a case but he's been a menace and I want to call a witness to the stand to prove such allegations." The D.A. spoke turning around scanning the crowd. When I noticed the look of surprise on Steve's face, I knew it was some shit in the game. The D.A. signaled for an older Hispanic lady to come to the stand. She looked to be in her late fifties. Her hair was grey with just a few black strands. It was shoulder length and curly. She used a cane to balance her movement. The lady was poorly dressed, yet her jewelry was exquisite.

I looked at Mun then at Steve and my heart begin to beat at a rapid speed. *Who the fuck is she?* I thought. The little lady took a seat on the stand as tears instantly fell from her eyes. The D.A. asked her a few questions about herself, and then cut to the case.

"How do you know Mr. Demonte Richards?" The D.A. asked the elderly lady giving her a stern look.

"Well, I don't actually know Mr. Richards but I've seen him before. My apartments St. Middleton has a laundromat and overnight when my grandkids were asleep, I snuck out to do a couple of loads of laundry. I was sitting on the bench in the Laundromat reading the Sunday's paper, when I saw that fella and another guy get out of a black vehicle toting big guns across their shoulder. Once they passed the rent office, I noticed them lift their weapons and I quickly ran and ducked behind the change machine. Seconds later, I heard the gunshots. It was as if the shooting went on for hours. When the shooting stopped and I was for sure they left, I took out running to check on my grandkids. I even left my clothes. I was just grateful to be alive. On my way home, I stepped over at least 10 dead bodies."

"Did you notice any one familiar? Steve asked.

"Yes, I did. Tears came to my eyes when I saw the young motionless bodies sprawled out on the compound. The kids ran around the apartments making all type of noises and stirring trouble, but they didn't deserve death."

I couldn't believe this old bitch was snitching, I thought.

"I object, your honor," Steve shouted.

"This woman is making this up. If these allegations are true, why didn't she go to the police when it first happened? Why wasn't she an eyewitness when they went door to door looking for anyone who had any information? Doesn't that mean she lied to law enforcements? Anyone who doesn't respect the law doesn't deserve to testify If she lied then; she'll lie now."

The judge slams his gavel. "Court is adjourned, and this hearing will be rest for further date."

I walked out of the Frank Crowley Court Building and spotted Donk standing outside his car waiting for me and Kadejah.

"Uncle Donk!" She screamed while she took off running in his direction. Even though Donk had been going back and forth to therapy, looking at him you couldn't tell he was ever paralyzed at one point. He sported a pair of peanut butter Timbs. His facial hair that he'd grown gave him a rugged look and the bullet he took to his left leg only added swagger to his walk. Looking into his eyes would scare you, because they were lifeless, but his smile would put you at ease. Until you realize he smiles even in the most serious situations.

When I first met him, he really creeped me out, but I've really grown to learn what type of person he is. He takes ruthless to a whole another level.

"They reset the court date again." I said as I hopped in the passenger seat.

"They what?" Donk responded with a mug on his face revealing his left gold tooth. He hopped in and slammed the car door. I didn't say anything, I just kept looking at him out the corner of my eye. The ride home was silent and awkward, but I was used to it. I swear if I wasn't in love with Mun and him and Donk wasn't related, I'll tell Donk to fuck my brains out. I loved his black

171

smooth skin. Although, I would never betray Mun like that. It don't hurt a bitch to dream right?

When we arrived to my house, I began to gather Kadejah's things.

"She's going with me. I'll drop her back off in a couple of hours." He said without even looking into my direction.

"Well, let me grab her some suit—"

"Whatever she needs, I'll just buy it while were out." He said cutting me off.

"Okay, call me when you're headed back this way."

"Bet."

CHAPTER 43
MUN

I can't believe this shit. This is the third time these bitches done reset my court. I laid on my bunk with my legs crossed at my ankles, and my hands placed underneath my head while I replayed every word the elderly lady said. I know it's some shit in the game because now that I remember, the washers and dryers inside of the Laundromat in St. Middleton don't even work and haven't worked in years. The young niggas were breaking down the machines and stealing all of the quarters, and everyone knows this! Somebody is trying to make sure I never make it up out this bitch, and the only person I know that will go to such extent is Lito. If I would've never got jammed up, I would've been murked his bitch ass, but I knew it won't be too long before Donk get his ass.

"Richards!" The officer yells standing on the other side of my cell.

"What's up?" I asked slightly lifting my head.

"Go to Medical."

I hopped off my bunk, slid on my black crocs and brushed my hair. Even on lock I kept myself on point. Niggas hated the fact I had so much swag. This was my favorite time of the day. As soon as the C.O. let me out my cell, I walked down the corridor to Medical. Danielle was sitting behind her desk waiting on a nigga.

This bitch was so fine. She had long thick natural eyelashes with light green eyes. Her hair was natural curly and black wand. I was obsessed with her big, juicy lips. Danielle had start working at the county jail after she graduated Med School and was naïve to a lot of street shit. Me and Danielle had been kicking it tough now for about six months.

"Hey baby." I spoke softly with a grin on my face as I eased the door closed behind me. Without looking away from the computer screen she said. "So, I still have to fuck my man at my job?"

"Look, I don't know what's going on but you know if I had a choice I would not be here."

"I know, daddy. I'm sorry I'm just so frustrated."

She walked from behind her desk and straddled my lap. She wore pink scrubs and even in her uniform you could see all her curves. I squeezed her ass cheeks and slid my tongue in her mouth kissing her slow and passionately. Moan's escaped her mouth as she began to plant soft kisses on my neck.

"You gon' stay down, right?" I asked pulling away from her embrace while I gazed into her eyes.

"Hell yeah, I'm not going nowhere!" With that being said, I pulled her shirt over her head exposing her perky D cup breast. I slowly removed one breast at a time as I flicked my tongue across her nipple. Her head fell back in ecstasy while I moved from one breast to the other.

"Uh un nigga, you teasing me" she said before hopping up and removing her pants. When I saw her neatly shaved pussy, I couldn't help but to smile. This bitch was so sexy. It wasn't a scrape or bruise on her body. Her thighs were thick and pretty and she had a red and black rose tattoo that started at her side and stopped right above her left knee. Before I knew it, my dick was standing at attention. She slowly walked toward me and slid off my pants as she dropped to her knees. She planted soft wet kisses all over my dick, making it disappear. She pulled it out and smacked her lips. She looks up at me while she massages and pulls on my dick right before she dives in and tease the tip, flicking her tongue around my hole and lightly sucking the tip. She grips my shaft tighter and goes in for the kill.

"Oooohhh shit, damn girl you go hard." I mumbled while biting down on my lip. The shit felt so good my eyes began to roll to the back of my head. I grip her head tighter and forcefully thrust my penis down her throat until I release in her mouth. Danielle swallowed my seeds and use her tongue to lick the remaining juices around her mouth.

"Um daddy you taste so—" A knock interrupts her, and we quickly scatter to get dressed bumping into each other and knocking things over in the process.

"Ms. Dominquez, you have an inmate out here that's in need of medical assistance." The male C.O. announced on the other side of the door. Danielle quickly grabs the ankle wrap out of the cabinet and pretends to wrap my ankle.

"You may enter." She yells while applying pressure to my ankle. As soon as the dude walks in, I immediately notice him as one of the dudes from my dorm. Off instinct, I mug the nigga and turn my attention back to Danielle. I couldn't help but to wonder if she fuck other niggas or is it just me. Yeah, the sex is good, but my bitch is at home. I wouldn't trade Bre for nothing in the world. I should change her name to loyalty, cause through it all she's been right by my side. Other than my sister and mother, she's my favorite lady. Danielle was single, so she claimed. I already informed her on what type of relationship we can have once I'm released, and if she want anything more than what I'm willing to give. I'm gon' chunk her ass the deuces.

"Okay Mr. Richards, I'll call you out tomorrow to see if the swelling has went down." She said before getting up and walking back to her desk shooting me a wink as she moved her attention to the computer screen. Without responding, I slowly rose from the seat and limped out the door not even acknowledging the dude sitting by the door waiting to be seen.

Ah'Million

CHAPTER 44
DONK

Shit was really becoming frustrating. I just can't understand why Mun hadn't been released. He supposed to been out. I'm constantly racking my brain trying to figure everything out. I was pretty upset yesterday, but today is a new day, I patiently waited outside of the county jail hoping to visit Mun. The sun is dwindling down, but it's still extremely hot outside, which don't bother me at all. The A/C in my whip blow like snowballs and my tint was as black as the color of my skin. I took one last toke of the blunt and put it out. I placed my phone inside of the glove compartment. As soon as I stepped out, sweat beads instantly formed across my forehead. Twenty minutes later, after going through the metal detector and identification verification process, I sat alone on a silver stool inside a small room. It had a plexiglass window used to separate me from the person on the other side. A few minutes pass and Mun walks in. I drop my head in agony before reaching for the phone.

"What's up, nigga?" Mun ask contently, putting me a bit at ease.

"Bruh, what's going on? Why you still in this bitch?" I ask frustrated.

"Man, I don't know, but a surprise witness testified against me yesterday and it threw me and Steve for a loop. So I'm assuming Steve needs more time."

"Who was the witness?"

"I don't know the lady. You have to call Jeff or Steve and ask one of them." Mun said covering the speaker on the phone.

"Okay. Other than that, you been alright? You need anything?"

"Nah, I'm just ready to get out and take over the streets again."

"You know fam I been thinking. The day I hit Sunny's spot, I dropped everything off at my spot. It should've been nothing in my car." I spoke with a perplexed look on my face.

"You must have forgotten those two or maybe picked them up from somewhere else earlier that day. It was something in the car. Steve showed me the evidence."

"Where were they at in the car?"

"The backseat."

"Nah, that's not even my steelo. That shit don't even sound right. I had hidden compartments all over that bitch. Why would I just dryly put two kilos in my backseat?"

"I don't know, fam. The shit sounded fraudulent to me too, but that was a year ago. It's nothing we can't do now, but continue to try and get me up out of here."

"You right. Maybe one of those pigs planted that shit, or maybe that nigga Lito. Regardless, I'm gon' handle that issue for you as soon as possible."

"Times up!" The CO yells. Mun quickly shoots me a glance of gratification and winks before finally pulling off. I was about to text Steve and Jeff to inquire about this new mystery witness, when I received an incoming text from Persuasia.

Persuasia: What you doing?

Me: Cooling, what's up?

Persuasia: Stop by the club ASAP I got some for you

Me: bet I'm omw

An hour later, I pull at KOD strip club. I shoot Persuasia a text letting her know I'm in the building. As soon as I looked up from my screen, we lock eyes as she grabs me by the arm leading me through the congested crowd. Some bitches were off to the side giving out private dances while two little petite bitches performed a routine onstage. Tonight, KOD was the place to be. Persuasia led me to the office door, and I quickly snatched my hand from her grip when I became hesitant of my surroundings.

"Where we going?" I asked pulling up my jeans ready for whatever.

"Boy calm down, it's a surprise for you crazy, and once you see it, you gon' thank me." She said smiling seductively. Her red lipstick complimented her straight white teeth and her tongue piercing made my man instantly hard. She wore a nude one-piece body suit revealing everything except her goodies. Persuasia opened the door to the office and led me inside. The room was spacious and neatly organized with a plasma TV built into the wall that displayed the clubs surveillances. Persuasia walked around the desk and I immediately begin to remove my sneakers.

"Whoah.... As bad as you want me, I want you, but this hit right here is better than pussy." Persuasia said pointing to something on the large screen. I lightly walked to the television and instantly my adrenaline begins to pump as I looked at her with a demoniac smirk. I turn my attention back to the screen inspecting each and every move.

"Damn girl, you really came through for a nigga. I owe you foreal." I stated surprised by Persuasia's devotion. She came and visited me at the hospital when I was on my nuts and I filled her in on the details, not once mentioning I needed her help. She took it upon herself to contact me.

"You don't owe my nothing, Donk. I just want you to know I'm down by law and since day one I wanted this bond to be more than just a fuck thang. I can smell bullshit but I know a real nigga when I see one, and since then, you had my nose wide open." I couldn't help but to stare at Persuasia as she spoke. Her hand rested on her hip and every so often she'll run her fingers through her hair seductively.

"My trust is a little fucked up, but this right here makes me see you in a totally different light. You not just another little shorty I'm fucking." I pulled her into my chest and gave her a long passionate kiss.

"Look, I'm gon' get you right later, but for now, go back to work. I need to watch my prey."

"Okay, daddy." She replied as she strutted out the office.

"Oh Persuasia, before you leave, give your farewells to your girls. Tonight is your last night." I know I counted all thirty-two of her teeth as she blushed uncontrollably, but I nonchalantly turned my attention back to the screen.

A few hours later, I quietly sit in front of the screen eyeing Lito and his men closely. To the naked eye he looks as if he's on point, but I've seen him guzzle at least four cups of Henny and Coke. A man can have the highest tolerance level but that Henny will put anyone on their ass. He may not be pissy drunk but he's drunk enough. I wonder what the occasion is. Lito signals to one of his men as he stands to his feet. I hop out of the seat and quickly grab my sneakers putting them on before rushing out of the door. I immediately spot Persuasia by the bar cursing at a dude who apparently touched her inappropriately.

"Persuasia!" I yell, but it's so loud that the music drowns out my voice. I sprint towards her and the dude and she jumps when she sees me. The dude is still in her face talking shit, obviously not noticing me approach them. My left fist connects with his chin and knocks him out cold.

"You ready?" I turn and ask Persuasia.

"Yeah, fuck this club!" She yells with her finger pointing toward the sky.

I grab her hand, stepping over the drunk dude's body that lay motionless on the ground before dashing towards the back door. I spot my forest green Jeep SRT and charge through the parking lot. The sound of Persuasua's heels clicking cause a few onlookers to look our way, but it didn't stop nor slow us down. I hit the alarm and hop in looking in every direction to make sure I don't lose Lito. Not even a minute pass before Lito and his two men exit the club. I press the start button in a black Range Rover. I wait patiently for them to pull off and exit the lot before I tail them.

Click! Click! The sound of the gun catches my attention instantly. I jerk my head in Persuasia's direction and see her checking the clip in her chrome 9mm handguns. I didn't know a female so cute and classy could be so gangsta. I may need to keep a keen eye on this bitch myself.

"How you know I was taking you with me?" I asked half joking.

"Oh, what you gone do? Put me out? I'm not going nowhere without you. You one deep but four hands is better than two." She replied without even looking into my direction. I slightly chuckle at the bravery. I just hope she knows what she doing.

For ten minutes, I've been two cars behind Lito. Thinking of easiest way to put this bastard out of his misery. I really regret bringing Persuasia along. Now I have to kill and protect all in one. Up ahead, Lito's black Range Rover veered into a gas station. The driver hops out and I pull into the gas station parking beside a gas pump on the opposite side.

"Look you go in and pay for the gas, try to lure the driver in."

"Okay." She responded before grabbing the handle and leaping out of the truck. Pesuasia strutted inside of the gas station while I kept my eyes on Lito's vehicle. I couldn't see inside due to the tint. But it didn't stop me from trying. I turned my focus to Persuasia as I watched her mingle with the dude that hopped out the driver seat of Lito's Range Rover.

She still had on the same clothes she wore at the club. I caught a glimpse of movement out of my peripheral vision and before I could reach for my Uzi, I felt the cold steel being pressed against my temple.

"Who sent you?" The man spoke through clenched teeth. I rested my hands on my lap without responding. If it's time, it's my time. I ain't begging' no nigga to spare me shit because if he anything like me, I'm good as dead.

"Come on, I got someone that wants to holler at you." He said as he discreetly shoved the pistol in my back, patting me down before guiding me toward Lito's car. As soon as I climbed in the backseat, I feel the burning sensation on the side of my temple from Lito's cigar. I tightened the muscles in my face to endure the suffering, because I knew this was only the beginning. The gunmen pushes me inside the truck causing me to stumble over before slamming the door shut.

"So, we meet again?" Lito asks keeping his focus ahead of him. I remain silent as I watch Persuasia walk round the store.

"This time you won't make it out alive, my boy."

"Why you still talking? Send me to my maker, nigga." I shot back.

Lito slightly chuckles "You're amusing. I like your sense of humor but we'll see who will have the final laugh.

I spotted Persuasia and the driver at the register. I'm sure they know she was with me, but I'm going to continue to hope she slipped through the cracks. Pesuasia staggers out of the store as if she had a couple of drinks. I'm sweating like a Hebrew slave with every step she takes toward the truck. My heartbeat quickens.

"Turn around man. Do not get in this truck." I recited over and over in my head. She was so busy impersonating a drunk woman that she never bothered to look over at the empty Jeep.

"I got a few friends with me, but once I drop them off you can ride up front with me." The driver lied to Persuasia as he walked her to Lito's side of the truck. As soon as the door opened, a confused look consumed Persuasia's face when she noticed me in the backseat. Before she could utter a word, the driver grabbed a fistful of her hair and shoved her inside the truck. We sat asshole tight, but before he closed the door, he snatched Persuasia's bag. I had my hopes up, as I recalled her placing the ratchet in her bag. Once the truck pulled off, I couldn't help but to notice Persuasia's wide eye expression.

"I'm gon' get us out this shit ma." I whispered with my head down. I can't believe I got caught slipping a second time. This shit ain't me. Persuasia pinched my thigh as she glanced at her crotch. I couldn't make out the hint until she mouthed the word *gun.*

"If one of you motherfuckas utter another word, I'm going to stain my windows with your brains." Lito spoke very calmly. Despite his calmness, I could sense the significance in his statement. He was ruthless but he was somewhat tipsy as well. The man seated behind us was really the only one totally sober. I begin to reflect on every way possible to snatch Persuasia's gun and murk these niggas. Suddenly, I hear a loud gagging noise from Persuasia's direction. She was bent over puking all over the place.

"You nasty bitch." The man behind her yells as he grabs her by her hair to lift her head. As soon as her heads jerks up, she aims the .38 at his throat. Boc! The bullet instantly makes his head burst and sends his body flying backwards. Boc! A direct shot to Lito's temple. Boc! A head shot to the driver which causes the truck to spin out of control and crash into a light post that made our bodies jerk forward. Persuasia shots were rapid and accurate and before I knew it, the bodies fell like a domino effect. They had all been hit before they could realize what was going on.

"Girl, what the fuck? Man girl you official!" I yelled with an incredulous expression on my face. I couldn't believe what had just transpired.

"It's a lot you have yet to learn about me." She smirked before aiming the gun at Lito's dead body. Boc! That's for Donk. Boc! And that's for me. Shorty was ruthless and I could tell it was going to be the beginning of something beautiful.

"Come on!" I yelled grabbing her by the arm. We hopped out the truck and begin sprinting towards the gas station where the Jeep was parked. Once we neared the gas station from a distance, I could see lights up ahead. Several armed police officers surrounded the truck.

"Did you have something illegal in the truck?" Persuasia asked out of breath as she rested her hands on her knees.

"Yeah, my Uzi." I shook my head in disgrace and pulled out my phone.

"Aye sis, come pick me up ASAP." I demanded hoping she was somewhere in pocket.

"Where you at? Are you okay?" she asked nervously.

"Yeah, I'm good. I'm on the side of Northwest Highway." I quickly informed.

"Okay, I'll call you when I get close." She assured.

I disconnected the call and immediately begin to look for a spot me and Persuasia could go unnoticed. Going back to the gas station was definitely out of the question.

"She on her way, bae?" Persuasia asked hesitantly. I could see a hint of fear in her eyes. I hadn't seen all night.

"Look mama, don't be afraid. Nothing is going to happen to you. I know you got a little man. If this shit happens to surface, I'm gon' take the rap. I'm a real nigga before I'm *anything* else." I assured her.

"Okay," she responded smiling and batting her eyelashes. She was so beautiful. Even after catching a whole body, she still looked gorgeous.

I grabbed her by her hand. "We have to lay on our stomach. It's nowhere to hide." I looked around once more before lying next to Persuasia. She hit the ground before I did. It was nothing prissy about her and I liked that shit. Minutes passed and we lay stagnant, awaiting Bre's arrival.

"Donk?" Persuasia whispered.

"Huh?"

"What's our next move?"

"Shit. We just gon' keep pushing. Don't worry about your job or no bullshit related to that issue. I'm a made nigga. Where yo lil man at right now?"

"He at my mom's. I usually pick him up when I get off work or early the next morning.

"Okay in the morn— "In mid-sentence, my cell phone lit up, cutting my conversation short. It was Bre.

"Hello?" I answered.

"I'm coming down Northwest Highway right now." She anxiously spoke sounding more nervous than me.

"I squinted my eyes, yet I saw no sign of Bre.

"I don't…wait, wait. Slow down right there. We crossing the street toward you." I ended the call and snatched Persuasia up by her arm. With the police diagonally across the street, we would have to be very discreet.

We quickly dashed across the street where Bre car was parked. We both hopped in the backseat. I wiped the beads of sweat that covered my forehead once I was seated.

"Where to?" Bre asked. I quickly sensed her attitude.

"Take me Rochelle's. Any other time, I would speak on her tone but I remained silent. I actually thought it was weird. She didn't seem upset when I spoke to her on the phone. I rubbed my chin as I began to think of anything that could've possibly pissed her off. I looked over at Persuasia and she was already knocked out with her head propped against the window. Shorty was more dangerous than I thought. *Who kills then sleep like it never happened?* I thought I was the only person who did that.

We drove pass the gas station and I noticed one of the officers inspecting the Uzi before placing it inside of a plastic bag. I knew shit would get real as soon as they found the three dead men inside the truck, but at least me and Persuasia will be on the other side of town. I happen to lock eyes with Bre through the rearview mirror and she was staring at me with a demented look in her eyes. I sat up the seat leaning in closely.

"What's up?" I whispered with a perplexed expression on my face.

"I'm good." She lied.

"Man I know you, girl. What's yo' problem?"

"Who?" I questioned in disbelief, stunned by her curiosity.

"Ol' girl in the backseat?"

"Why?" I couldn't believe what I was hearing.

"I'm just trying to figure out what's going on." She lied.

I could see a twinge of jealousy in her eyes so I just sat back and refused to utter another word. What the fuck is she questioning me for? Bitches ain't shit.

Ah'Million

CHAPTER 45
BRE

Me and Kadejah stood in the line at the Family Dollar purchasing socks and underwear for Mun. I was so ready for him to come home. It really bothered me last night to see Donk still doing the same shit, living the same life. I thought he would have gotten his mind right with Mun being gone, due to his bullshit at that. The store was packed as usual. I hated coming to the hood, but I decided to grab him a few things along the way. I stood waiting impatiently behind a heavy-set lady. It looked as if she had a hundred hair rollers in her head and her robe was three times her size. She was so busy cursing at her children that she didn't realize the cashier was done scanning all of her items.

"Mm-humm." I cleared my throat.

"Ma'am she's ready," I spoke in a polite tone avoiding eye contact, hoping she wouldn't be offended by my comment. She quickly turned around and sized me up, placing one hand on her hip.

"Baby, I don't need you telling me a damn thang!" She yelled as her left eye begin to jump. Everyone in the store got quiet and directed their attention toward me and the lady. I was so embarrassed; this would have never happened in the suburbs.

"Don't talk to my momma like that!" Kadejah yelled as her veins protruded from her neck. She balled her fist and held them wisely by her side.

"And who you?" Before she could finish her sentence, I raised my hand cutting her off.

"Fuck this shit." I mumbled throwing the underwear and socks on the counter. I grabbed Kadejah's hand, threw my hair over my shoulders and strutted out of the store. The sun beams attacked me as soon as I exited the store. I hated the month of August. It was scorching hot. Summer never been one of my favorite seasons. I could tell Kadejah was still upset by her silence. She was always so bubbly and talkative. I hope Mun would be alright with me bringing him his things another day. It's not like he needed them. I make sure he has plenty. I just did not have the patience to deal with that lady any longer. I hit alarm on my 2016 purple Nissan Altima. Me and Kadejah got into the car and pulled out the parking spot. As I sped through the parking lot, I noticed the big lady and her children walking out of the store.

"Tramp!" The little boy hollered cupping his hands over his mouth to enhance his volume. I just chuckled and kept it moving.

"Mama?" Kadejah asked looking at me with piercing eyes. You could tell she had something on her mind.

"Yes baby?" I replied placing my hand on top of hers to let her know she had my undivided attention.

"Um…Why didn't you fight that lady when she did that to you?" My eyes widened and I sneered at her question.

"Fight?" I asked with a flustered look on my face. I couldn't believe she just asked me something so displeasing.

"Why should I have fought, Kadejah?" Not giving her too much time to respond.

"Well um… She paused as she looked down and began to fidget in the seat.

"My uncle Donk told me if someone disrespect me, to handle my business." She mocked. I couldn't believe Donk would tell her something so violent. I'm making a mental note to curse his ass out as soon as I leave from visiting Mun.

"Kadejah, everything does not have to be solved with violence. Some things you have to just walk away from. Listening to your uncle Donk, you will end up in the same place as your Uncle Mun.

"Okay, mama." She responded then directed her attention out the window. *I'm really going to have to let Donk ass have it*, I thought while pulling into parking lot of the county jail.

Mun walked into the visiting room with an orange jumpsuit on. Even in the dull attire, he was so enticing. His hair was neatly lined up and freshly faded on the sides. I could tell by his arms, he'd gained a few pounds of muscle. As soon as he spotted me and Kadejah, his face lit up like a Christmas tree and he quickly picked up the phone. I hated this behind the glass shit. I was in need of some affection.

"Hey, baby," he said while smiling and waving at Kadejah. It was only one phone per booth. I handed the phone to Kadejah and allowed her to talk to Mun while I strolled to the vending machines. The loud noise of my heels clicking with each step caused a lot of people to look my way. I was use to the attention. My Tru Religion jeans hugged my ass. I placed the Versace clutch underneath my arm as I strutted even harder to give the CO's something to look at. I grabbed a ham and cheese sandwich for Mun, Animal Crackers for Kadejah and a bag of Flamin' Hot Cheetos for myself. When I bent the corner, I peeped my head back inside the room where Mun and Kadejah looked as if they were having the time of their life.

"Snacks!" Kadejah yelled hopping off the stool, running toward me with her arms stretched out in front of her.

"Stop acting like you not used to nothing." I whispered before handing the CO Mun's sandwich to give to him.

So, what's going on with you?" I asked Mun while the payphone rested on my shoulder.

"I got some good news."

"What?" I asked eyes the size of golf balls.

"This morning we went to speedy trial. I found out the witness that spoke against me last week refused to testify at my next hearing, and on top of all that she denies all allegations."

I couldn't believe what I was hearing. I wanted to scream at the top of my lungs. I reached over and squeezed Kadejah's hand. I was so excited.

"But wait. Won't she get in trouble for that?"

"Yep and she is."

"That's weird, but it doesn't even matter. So, when exactly are you coming home?"

"Steve said I'll be released on probation one day this week." I could tell by Mun's face expression that he was relieved, yet content. There were no worries in his eyes.

"I miss y'all. I can't wait to come home," Mun said while looking past me. He quickly diverted his attention back to me, but I noticed the uneasiness in his eyes. I turned around and spotted the woman pass the booth. Her hair was long and curly. She looked bi-racial but she was beautiful. She turned around meeting me gaze as she smirked before strolling down the hallway. I quickly turned my attention towards Mun.

"You fucking her?" I asked with squinted eyes. He threw his hands up hysterically as if my question was irrelevant.

"Man come on Bre, don't do that. I mean she's cute but how am I gone fuck that woman? I'm in orange, this ain't no movie shit. This real-life. Shit don't go down lie that here."

I guess I'll drop it. I can't prove it and to be honest, he's right. It's no ways they can have sex anyways without someone seeing something. One thing I do know… time tells everything.

"Um okay, I hear you nigga." I replied rolling my eyes.

"Time's up!" The C.O. yelled.

"I love y'all." Mun states giving me an air kiss while throwing Kadejah hearts. "I'll see y'all soon!" He shouted from behind the glass.

"Uncle Mun, is I'm still gon' get my ice cream you promised?" Kadejah yelled out. Mun slightly chuckled as he headed back to his dorm. I stood in the booth until I could no longer see Mun's shadow. I slowly turned around, grabbing Kadejah by the hand as we made our exit.

"Mama somebody at the door!" Kadejah shouted. It wasn't no one but Donk. I called him after I left the jail and told him I needed to speak to him. I was standing over the stove cooking mashed potatoes, sweet potatoes, meatloaf, and green beans when Kadejah called my name. I wiped my hands on my apron and headed towards the door, stepping over Kadejah's toys along the way. I unlocked the door, inviting Donk inside. As soon as he walked past me, I caught a whiff of his Chanel Bleu cologne. I guess today was just a typical day for him. He wore a white tank top, light denim Levi shorts, with a pair of Gucci flip flops. His 24ct gold rope necklace hung to the middle of his chest, and his pinky ring had so many diamonds in it. If you didn't know him, you probably would think it was fake.

"Damn sis, it smell good in here." He said jokingly as he looked around.

"Where Kadejah?" He asked.

"She was just right there."

"Boo!" Kadejah yelled jumping from behind the couch. Laughter escaped his lips as he grabbed her lifting her small body into the air. I let them enjoy each other's presence as I slid past them, walking back to the stove. I know I have to be calm as possible bringing the issue up with Donk. At the end of the day, he's not my nigga. Mun is. A few minutes pass and Donk slowly strolls into the kitchen. On the cool, this fool low key arrogant.

"What's up sis?" He asked with a concerned expression on his face, but I wanted him to feel where I was coming from so I inched a few steps closer.

"Donk". I paused slowly inhaling before speaking.

"Today, I got into an altercation with a lady and Kadejah told me that you told her to fight if someone disrespect her." Donk smirked and began to rub his chin as he slowly bobbed his head up and down in approval while keeping his eyes directed at the floor. He slowly raised his head up to meet my gaze. The deranged look in his eyes told me to stop while I was ahead and walk away, but I refused to back down. His silence was killing me and I know he peeped it once I began to fidget. I wanted him to say something already. The longer I stood there, I became more and more apprehensive of his next move.

"Say Bre," he slowly spoke as he motioned towards me, barely lifting his tank top that exposed his red boxer briefs.

"Don't you ever call me on some urgent shit in regard to what the fuck I tell my niece? Quaylo is her mother, that's my mother-fucking blood." Even though calm as ever, his words came out so trenchant. It was if those little beady eyes were looking into the depths of my soul.

"I understand, but I just don't want her to grow up with things like that instilled in her." I calmly stated placing my hand on my hip. Donk looked me up and down before grabbing his car keys off the table. Without a word being said, he grabbed the crotch of his jeans and motioned out of the kitchen.

"Where you going?" I asked looking astonished following behind him. "Donk," I yelled snatching his hand. He turned his head in my direction and stared me down for what seemed like hours before walking through the house. Before stepping into the living room, I ran and jumped in front of him to attain his attention. Donk had a very domineering aura and his presence made me feel some type of way.

"Look, Bre. You really don't know what type of nigga I am. So until you figure it out, only call me if it has something to do with my brother or my niece." He took a step forward, but stopped in mid-stride once he realized I wasn't moving. I couldn't hold my composure any longer. I lunged forward and wrapped my arms around his neck inching closer until our lips met. With the quickness, Donk removed my arms from around his neck with force while looking at me in bewilderment.

"You foul dog. Move, watch out!" He yelled roughly pushing me out of the way. "You disloyal bitch!" He called out lifting Kadejah from the floor and placing her into his arms.

"We gone. I'll bring her back later on," he said before walking out of the house. I didn't even bother to say anything back. I felt so humiliated and ashamed. I know I fucked up big time. What's even more fucked up is he didn't even react the way I wanted him too. I just hope he keep's that episode between us.

CHAPTER 46
DONK

Me and Kadejah sat side by side at the ice cream shack on Eleventh Street. Even though the shack was small, the ice cream was homemade and delicious. Since a kid, my mother used to bring me, Quaylo, and Mun here all the time. I try to keep myself busy as possible because every time I sit still, I think about my mother and sister. I missed them dearly. When I was a kid, my deepest fear was death. Only because I was told when I get to Heaven, I will no longer know my family. With the deaths of my mother and sister, I realize what I feared most isn't so frightening and it's hard to fear the inevitable. Loosing Quaylo never came to mind. I know eventually everyone has to die, because you get old with time, but shit always happens when you least expect it. She left behind a beautiful little girl and I plan to love and protect her just as I did with her. I've already mentally made my decision. No more malicious killing and robbing. Those days are over. I wish Rochelle was here to see me now.

"Unc?" Kadejah called out looking up at me with her big bedroom eyes. Her ponytail looked a bit messy because she cried when Persuasia tried combing her hair. I let her hair keep her hair the way it was. One night at my house turned into two and I enjoyed every minute of it.

"Can I stay with you one more time?" She asked with puppy dog eyes.

"You mean one more day?" I asked correcting her.

"Yes! I just love ice cream, Uncle Donk. Thank you so much for bringing me here." She babbled continuously.

"You welcome, niecy." I stated grabbing her by her hand and guiding her toward the door. I held the door open for her as I walked closely behind. Once outside, she took off towards my white 2016 300 Chrysler. Me and Persuasia went to the dealer and copped it a few days ago. As soon as I opened the passenger door, my phone began to ring. I walked to the other side of the car and hopped in.

"Wassup baby?" I answered.

"Bae, on your way home can you stop by the store and pick me up some aspirins. I'm not feeling too good," Persuasia stated trying to sound sexy, low key enticing a nigga. Ever since I moved her and her little man in, shit been going pretty smooth. She down as fuck and she don't be with all the extra shit. She was attending school full time with no worries.

"Alright bet. I'm 'bout to go holler at Lil Tim to see if he good." I replied pulling out of the lot. Since rehabilitating from the incident, me and Lil Tim have become a team. I gave him ten of the twenty bricks that I snatched from Sunny and we been doing our thing. Keeping shit up and running while Mun on lock and taking care of his business as well.

"Okay. Baby, is Kadejah still with you?" She asked curiously.

"Yes." I responded.

"Boy, you hell." She slightly chuckled. She already knew how I felt about Kadejah. My shorty move when I move and go where I go and bet not nobody fuck with her.

"You know how we do it." I responded with a grin on my face looking over at Kadejah who was bobbing her head to the music. She was my pride and joy. Ever since I found out she was my niece, I've been making wiser moves. With Quay being gone, me and Mun is all she got.

"Bye boy"

"Alright." I ended the call and placed my phone inside the cup holder before turning up the volume to Lil Kodak's latest hit. To Mun's knowledge, I was stopping by the spot daily making sure Lil Tim was running shit smoothly, but I decided against the idea. Lil' Tim was sixteen years old now and it was time for him to step up to the plate. Since Rico been gone, Lil Tim been moving all the weight. I would just drop by occasionally to pick up and drop off and make sure everything counted for and nothing is out of order With Lito being out of the picture, the dope wasn't as pure nor cheap, but regardless I was making sure Mun shit was straight. Mun felt as if Lil Tim was too young, but I was underestimated at a young age as well. It was easy for me too relate to the lil nigga.

194

If you ask me, he was doing a damn good job for his age. A few minutes later, I pulled up on Lil Tim at the spot. He was sitting outside with the driver door open to his metallic grey Grand Marquis.

While his left leg hung out, he was so busy jamming he hadn't even notice me parked in front of the house. I turned the volume down and watched him closely.

"I should scare his ass." I said out loud.

"Uncle Donk, is that Little Tim? Kadejah asked struggling to see over the dashboard.

"Yeah, that's his ass over there slipping."

"Oooh, can you let me out. He told me he was gone give me some money for my birthday!" She exclaimed, unbuckling her seatbelt. I just shook my head and looked at her bad ass. This little girl was always looking for a come up.

"Alright, sneak out and go scare him." I suggested.

"You talking 'bout sshhhh?" She asked placing her index finger over her mouth.

"Yeah, sshhh. Be very quiet." I joked. I leaned over and pushed her door open to give her enough space to slide out.

A burst of laughter escaped my mouth as I watched Kadejah crouch down and ease towards Lil Tim. What the hell do she know about getting down like that? I'm gone have to ask her a couple of questions when we get back to the house. When Kadejah reached out and touched Lil Tim's leg, he jumped so hard his shin hit the bottom of the door. I was reclined back in my seat with tears in my eyes filled with laughter.

His facial expression quickly softened once he saw Kadejah's face. He picked her up and walked towards the car.

"Nigga, you play too much!" He yelled jokingly. I hopped out the car and met him halfway. He put Kadejah down as we dapped up. He wore a burgundy Burberry V-neck shirt, khaki Burberry shorts with the burgundy calf skin Burberry loafers.

"You good nigga?" I asked walking towards the porch.

"Yeah, everything is everything. I got that for you in the house. Lil Tim was a youngin' that I respected. He had a hustle

195

about himself and he wasn't saving up for the hottest designer clothes or shoes. He was just a regular hood nigga. He wore his dreads into a low ponytail with his baseball cap pulled down low barely revealing his eyes. His dimples and baby face would make you question his gangsta, but the lil nigga was really about that action. Kadejah tugged at Lil Tim's pocket.

"Wassup, Kadejah?" He joked already knowing what she wanted. Kadejah didn't even respond, she just stuck her hand out. Lil Tim reached into his pocket and peeled off a few twenties, placing them into Kadjeah's hand.

"You stay hitting a nigga up." Lil Tim laughed.

"Thank you, Little Tim" she spoke in the sweetest voice. We stepped inside the spot, and Lil Tim headed straight to the back. I glanced around the house to see if everything was straight. A sheet over the windows in place of curtains and a blanket hung atop, separating the living from the kitchen. Pyrex pots and scales sat in the corner with an air mattress reclined against the wall, but shit looked pretty tight. I examined the place a bit more, because you can never be too sure. A few minutes pass and Lil Tim walks from the back holding a Chick-Fil-a bag. He hands me the bag I and I pull a stack out and thumb through it before placing the money back into the bag.

"You haven't found a new connect yet, fam?" Lil Tim asks me before flopping down on the sofa. Me and Kadejah remained standing. I didn't want to get comfortable in a place like this with her.

"Nah, I haven't. To be honest I haven't really been looking for one. We just gon' have to stick to the nigga we got until I find us someone new. I'm gon' get on it ASAP." I stated walking towards the door. Lil Tim slowly eased himself off the sofa and trailed behind us out the door. He stood on the porch watching us leave from a distance.

"Hit me up fam!" He yelled out behind us. I nodded in approval right before he turned around and entered the house.

Memories of the day I almost died resurfaced when I pulled up to a red light that was seconds away from everything that took place. Since the whole incident, I've had my doubts and concerns because I'm precise about everything I do and I'm not the one to ride around with dope in my backseat. The shit just didn't make sense. The sound of horns behind me startled me from my thoughts. I sped through the light and veered into the gas station.

I was gunned down in the middle of the street directly in front of this exact gas station.

"Uncle Donk, can I go in too? Kadejah asked eagerly.

"Yeah and you don't have to ask me stuff like that. When I move, you move. Remember that." I assured her before opening the door. I don't know how Kadejah's foster parents were but I could tell they weren't nice. It was a good thing we never met. Me and Kadejah walked hand in hand into the store. The store was pretty empty besides the people that sat at the slot machines. Kadejah instantly took off running around the store picking up shit, but I wasn't going to stop her. I would've bought her the whole gas station if she asked for it. I could smell the fishy aroma coming from the left part of the mini food court. The fish basket looked pretty appealing but Persuasia will have a fit if I buy this carryout after hours of her slaving over the stove. I noticed a short and corpulent Indian dude walk from the back. He looked as if he was wearing a tupee and he had a very thick mustache.

"Come in, Kadejah." I said waving my hand.

"Bring what you got up here. It's time to go!" I yelled. Kadejah rounded the corner with so many snacks that shit was falling and hitting the floor with every step. Juice, hard candy, chocolate, chips. You name it, she had it. I just stood back and watched her in awe. I love to see her smile. As quickly as one item fell, she'll pick it up. Then BAM! Another one hit the floor.

"I'm coming, Unc!" She called out struggling to carry all of her things. I finally decided to help her.

"Uh un, I got it." She protested steady struggling. To my surprise, she managed to pick up all her things at once and slowly made her way to the register.

"You need my help now?" I asked her once I noticed she realized she wasn't tall enough to sit the things on the counter. She nodded in approval and I grabbed everything and sat it on the countertop. I watched the dude intensely while he rang up the items debating whether or not to peek my curiosity.

"$14.86." He announced.

"Give me a bottle of Aspirins, too." I stated pointing towards the wall behind him. I handed him a twenty dollar bill and grabbed the bags off the counter. I paused, giving Kadejah time to walk in front of me and lead the way, but something in my gut stopped me in mid stride.

"Hold on, Kadejah." I declared directing my focus on the dude behind the register.

"Aye, can I ask you something?" I asked with squinted eyes.

"Sure." He stated with a serious expression on his face.

"Do you remember the incident that took place in front of your store about a year ago?" I questioned. He paused momentarily as he took time to think.

"A black car, little girl. Several shots were fired." I continued.

"Oh yes, yes, yes. I remember." He replied swiftly.

"Um…not that I remember. Like what? It was all out of the ordinary if you ask me."

"Did you see a policemen or by stander put anything inside the car?"

"Which car? It was two black ones."

"The car the dude was shot in."

"Um nooo." He said dragging his words while he continued to rack his brain.

"Wait, wait, there was a female." He pointed jabbing his finger into the air looking past me as if he was in deep thought. "Yes it was a lady." He screeched.

"Did she put something inside the car?" I inquired as my heart begin to beat rapidly.

"Yes, a black bag. It looked more like a fast food to go bag, or a shopping bag. I couldn't tell."

"Did you see her car? Do you know show she look?"

"I do not remember the car, but I do know she was a black lady." I peeled off a few hundred-dollar bills and handed it to him.

"Preciate ya." I stated grabbing Kadejah's hand walking out of the store. My mind was racing a mile a minute as I tried to decipher what bitch would set me up. I can't believe someone had the audacity to set me up, and now my brother locked up paying for the shit.

Ah'Million

CHAPTER 47
MUN

I sat on the metal bench in book out awaiting my release. I'm so glad this shit is over with. I'm not used to sitting still for so long. Minutes pass and I wait patiently for them to process me out. The system takes twenty minutes to book you in, but twenty hours to release you. My train of thought was interrupted when I saw Danielle bend the corner. She had a clipboard in her hand while she stopped and spoke to one of the COs. I see her point towards my direction and I sat up attentively on the bench. She slowly strutted towards me. Danielle was so attractive.

"Mr. Richards," she stated looking around swiftly to make sure no one was watching.

"You have my number, right?" She asked looking down at the clipboard.

"Yeah." I slyly grin.

"Okay, make sure you call me as soon as you get the chance. I have something for you." She winked before walking away. I couldn't wait to beat her back out without having to sneak and creep. That shit was wack to me, but I can't complain. At least, I was getting some pussy. You had some niggas bussin open and penetrating oranges.

"Right this way, Mr. Richards," the CO shouted. I leaped off the bench and followed him down the long corridor. With each step, I could smell my freedom and I became more and more anxious. We came to a stop in the middle of the vestibule as he handed my property.

"Walk out that door straight ahead of ya and you're a free man." He stated.

"Country ass motherfucka." I mumbled as I sprinted out the front door. As soon as my feet hit the pavement, I squinted my eyes from the direct sunlight. I grinned from ear to ear as I looked around for my people.

"Mun." A voice called out. When I looked to my left, I saw Donk, Bre and Kadejah standing beside a white 300 Chrysler. I quickly jogged towards them feeling ecstatic. Kadejah ran to me first and hugged my kneecap. I lifted her off her feet and planted kisses all over her face.

"I missed you, Uncle Mun! She yelled delighted as she wrapped her arms around my neck. "I missed you too, baby girl." I said placing her on my hip while I passionately kissed Bre. She looked exquisite with her long maxi dress and her neatly polished toenails that were easily exposed in her gold MK sandals.

"My nigga, my nigga." Donk expressed while shaking my hand. I looked him up and down and after eating all those bullets, it wasn't a stain on him.

"You looking good, nigga" I said as we walked in unison to the car.

"What was you in there doing? Lifting weights? You look like an action figure." He joked.

Two hours later, Donk and I sat at the dinner table in the small apartment. I rented the space a couple of months before I got locked away for extra space to store my extra money and dope. While we sat conspiring our next move, Donk informed me about the new information he had received from a witness the day he got shot. I felt in my heart the setup had something to do with Lito.

Do you think Lito had something to do with it? I asked. Donk looked at me with a perplexed expression as if I had just spoke in a foreign language.

"I didn't tell you?" He asked.

"Tell me what?"

"Persuasia murked Lito and two of his boys about a week ago." He replied confidently.

"Whaaaatttttt?" I was astonished. I would've never imagined shorty to be a gangsta. Donk slowly nodded in approval, while slyly grinning. It was crazy the shit that actually aroused him. He has finally found him a female that would literally kill for him. Donk rose to his feet and walked to the back, only to return with a black bag.

"This right here is half of everything since the day you got jammed. I had Lil Tim in charge of damn near everything." He stated handing me the bag before taking a seat on the sofa.

"Yeah, I'm gon' link up with Lil Tim later on. I think he's going to be the one to replace Rico. I already know you gon' get back to doing you."

"Actually bro, I think I want to be your right hand man. I'm not trying to do nothing that will jeopardize me losing or leaving Kadejah. She need me just like Quay needed me, and I'm gone make sure nothing happens to her." He spoke humbly. I never thought I'll see the day Donk put his ski mask up. He despised hustlers and disagreed with the whole operation.

"I'm glad you got ya head on straight. I know the dope game is still a gamble, but it's less of a risk. I'm running my shit tight and right." I said kicking my feet up. Donk and I chatted for what seemed like hours until we had everything figured out.

I filled him in on my fling with Danielle as I reached into my pocket and showed him a picture of her.

"Jail pussy? You bet not let Bre find out. Shorty fine as hell though." He commented.

"What you got planned for the night?" He asked.

"I'm gon' just chill with Bre and Kadejah at yo' spot for a lil bit before I head to the crib. Persuasia always want a nigga at the crib, but I don't mind cause she keep a nigga right."

"That's what's up. Shit, let's go."

I could smell the food as soon as I stepped through the door. Kadejah had toys sprawled across the floor of the living room and she wasn't even nowhere to be found.

"Bre!" I called out stepping over the toys as I followed the delicious smell. Donk and I walked into the kitchen and I spotted Kadejah sitting on top of the counter while Bre stood beside her washing the dishes.

"Hey," they both called out. Kadejah was smiling from ear to ear. I could see the silver caps that a dentist placed on her back teeth.

203

"Kadejah, Uncle Donk here." I announced before Donk leaped from the side of the refrigerator. She quickly squirmed off the counter and jumped down with ease running into Donk's arms. I loved seeing Bre in her cooking apron. She looked so enticing. I walked up on her and pressed my erection against her apple bottom while I wrapped my arm around her waist.

"Alright, don't start nothing you can't finish," she said seductively as she spun around staring directly into my eyes. I passionately kissed her lips and slapped her on the ass as I turned to walk off.

"Where you going?" She pouted.

"Damn, girl." I chuckled. "Can a nigga go take a piss?" I laughed shaking my head as I continued down the hall. I walked into my bedroom and grabbed my jeans I had worn home from the county. I swiftly looked in the pockets and retrieved the small sheet of paper that Danielle's number was written on. I repeated the number out loud a few times before placing the sheet of paper back into my pocket. I treaded lightly to the restroom and dialed Danielle's number as I turned the volume down on the phone.

"Hello," she answered.

"Wassup girl, this Mun."

She gasped then said. "Hey baby. I missed you. Where you at? When you coming to see me?" She asked impatiently.

"What you doing tomorrow?"

"You." She snickered.

"Okay. Bet. Text me an address and I'm gon' come scoop you tomorrow." I assured.

"Okay. I'll be waiting."

With that being said, I ended the call. As soon as I opened the door to the restroom, Bre stood directly in front of me with her hands on her hips. *Damn, I haven't been home 24 hours and I done got caught already,* I thought until she wrapped her arms around my neck and began to kiss me like she'll never see me again. I wrapped my arms around her waist and deeply kissed her back. She paused and looked up into my eyes.

"Fuck me, Mun." She whispered aggressively tugging at my Ralph Lauren cargo shorts.

"Right now while Kadejah and Donk here?" I asked.

"Yes, right now. Kadejah is with Donk. Just a quickie. Please, I need you inside of me now." She begged.

Without even responding, I commenced to tearing Bre's clothes off. We were like dogs in heat. Once Bre was fully undressed, I stood back as I examined her body from head to toe. She was built like a stallion. Her honey colored skin glowed exposing her smooth physique. Before I knew it, I roughly grabbed Bre and turned her around.

"Arch your back." I whispered in her ear before whipping my man out. I inserted an inch at a time slowly easing myself inside of her juice box. Her pussy was tight and wet. She stood on the tips of her toes to give me a better access to her pussy. I used one hand to muffle the uncontrollable moans that escaped her mouth. Once she got used to the size, she slightly arched her back and gyrated her hips back and forth as if she wanted to feel the dick in her stomach. Her walls became snug and tight and I could tell she was about to bust. I dug myself deeper into her, building up my own release point.

"Mun! Mun!" she whispered loudly. "Oh Mun, baby I'm coming! Go deeper! Deeper! She cried out right before she exploded. I then released my warm cream inside of her. I pulled out and kissed her lips.

"I missed you, daddy." She stated breathing heavily.

"I missed you too." I shot back as I began to get dressed.

"Look bae, I'm 'bout to go holla at my bro before he leaves." I said leaving her to finish getting dressed. I walked into the living room to find it surprisingly empty.

"Donk!" I shouted looking around as I walked towards the front door. I looked out the window to find Donk's car no longer in the driveway. When I shut the door, I spotted a little small note at the end of the sofa.

"I know this your first day home. I got Kadejah. Do ya thang. You can slide through and pick her up tomorrow." I balled up the small sheet of paper while laughing to myself.

"Bre!" I yelled. Shit was about to get real.

***

The sun peeked through the blinds as Bre and I lay in the bed of our two-story home. I awoke to find Bre lying naked on top of the sheets. A smile spread across my face. It was good to be home. I sent a small prayer to the heavens. Man I was glad to be home. I planted a kiss on Bre's forehead before sliding out of bed. I walked around the house without a care in the world. Ass naked, dick swinging. Something I couldn't and wasn't going to do while I was incarcerated. After taking a quick shower and getting dressed, I walked into the bedroom and slapped Bre on the ass cheeks.

"Wake up, ma. Make a nigga some to eat. Some breakfast or something." I spoke standing over Bre. She instantly eased out of bed and went inside the restroom. A couple minutes later, she steps out with her pink robe tired at her waist and proceeds to the kitchen. I shoot Lil' Tim a quick text letting him know I'll be stopping by the spot to rap with him in about an hour. I could already smell the bacon and eggs coming from downstairs. I quickly sent a text to Danielle.

ME: GM beautiful

Danielle: Hey daddy

Me: I'm coming to get you around 1 pm be ready

Danielle: Ok

I placed my phone into my back pocket and grabbed a few stacks out of the bag Donk gave me yesterday. I headed to the kitchen where the tasty aroma was coming from and took a seat at the bar.

"It's beef bacon, scrambled eggs, grits, maple and honey sausage and waffles." Bre said as she handed me my plate. She poured me a cup of juice to wash it all down. I tried to take my time with the meal but after a couple of bites, I began to devour the food like a wolf who hadn't eaten in days. Once I finished off the plate, I walked behind the counter where Bre stood and pulled her into my arms.

"Bre, you know I got to make a couple of runs, but just hit me whenever you need me." I spoke with assurance referring to me and Lil Tim's meeting as well as linking up with Danielle's fine ass. I was gone show her what it's like to chill with a real nigga, but not before I rap with Lil Tim. Donk informed me on how the young nigga stepped all the way up to the plate when I got knocked. I probably would've never thought to give him such position. At times, I happen to think about Rico. Shit really happened fast, but what bothered me most was the fact he killed Quaylo. What made him do that?

I guess I'll never know.

I've always been the one to show love. Niggas also knew not to test my gangsta. I aint Rich Homie but I keep me a couple hittas. With Donk being home, I'd been waiting on a pussy to test me. Won't nobody make a better example than him? I hung around the spot a little longer with Lil Tim discussing business before finally deciding to leave.

"Hold it down fam. I'm gon' hit you up tomorrow." I promised as I headed out the front door. Lil Tim followed me out the house. I paused a few minutes to take a look at the ongoing traffic, nothing seemed out of order. I was used to the stares from the bitches across the way. I knew every hood bitch dream. I took out my phone and dialed Danielle number as I hopped in my Denali truck.

"I'm on my way. Be ready." I stated as soon as she picked up her phone.

"I'm already dressed and ready waiting on daddy." She replied sounding hella sexy. I let out a slight chuckle.

"Okay, give me ten minutes." I said hoping I can keep my dick in my pants.

***

Danielle stayed up north in an area called Mesquite, outside of Dallas. The neighborhood was extremely quiet. The yards were neatly cut and trimmed. It almost reminded me of my neighborhood. I made a left onto her street and immediately noticed her standing in her driveway. The strong breeze caused her sundress to blow wildly, revealing enough to arouse my imagination. I pulled into the driveway and watched her strut towards my truck. I opened the door and hopped out. We hugged and slowly kissed. The sweet scent of her perfume aroused me even more.

"Oooohhhh baby, I missed you. I'm so glad you're free and we can do shit our way." She said as she pulled away and gazed into my eyes. Danielle was by far one of the sexiest women I ever ran across. You see her type on music videos and reality shows. But I wasn't going to let her know how much of an effect her beauty had on me. It was no point. Yes I love me a beautiful bitch but loyalty is what keeps me, and any sign of disloyalty will get you cut off forever. I kissed her passionately while I squeezed her soft ass, only to discover she had nothing on underneath her dress. I felt my man begin to rise.

"Come on, get in." I said releasing my grip. I couldn't help but to watch her ass jiggle as she bypassed me and walked to the other side of the truck. We slowly cruised the streets of Dallas laughing and getting well acquainted. In the county, we were so bent on having sex we barely spent any time getting to know one another. I pulled into the lot of the Galleria Mall. We walked hand in hand through the lot. Bystanders glanced into our direction as we giggled and talked like a teenage couple. Danielle had a rare sense of humor. She was so naïve to certain things so all of her concerns and responses were so amusing.

"I know you've been here before, but today everything is on me. Go pick up whatever you like." I directed once we entered the store.

"Okay." She smiled flattered by my request. Without hesitating, Danielle walked into the Gucci store and picked out a few bags, leaving me with a tab of $2600. She went from store to store, Louis Vuitton, Victoria Secret, Chanel Bakers, Aldo's, just throwing it in the bag. I knew a few of Danielle's secret that she had in her closet, but with the help of my old bunky, I found out some things I would definitely need to know. So this little investment is nothing. Her little shopping spree had finally come to an end. I walked up behind her and carefully pressed my erection against her soft ass. She was trying on a pair of Dolce and Gabana shades.

"If you want him, I advise you to hurry up." Without responding, she quickly carefully placed the shades back on the rack and seductively looked back at me before prancing out of the store.

Bre had been blowing up my phone even after I answered my phone and reassured her on my whereabouts. She continued to call although I was giving her the benefit of the doubt. Now, I just don't give a fuck. I would turn my phone completely. After Danielle cooked hot water cornbread, cabbage mac and cheese, green beans, steak and potatoes we had mind blowing sex. This was the first time I made love to her. I showed every part of her body the attention it deserved. The love making session lasted for hours and now we lay on our back covered in sweat. She rested her head on my arm as I lay on my back contemplating my next move. The smell of sex fill the room, while her Jagged Edge CD played at a low volume on her laptop. I slowly sat up, startling Danielle from whatever she was thinking about.

"What's wrong?" She asked grabbing the blanket that lay by her feet to cover her exposed body.

"Nothing, I'm good ma." I lied looking deeply into her eyes.

"I really enjoyed myself today, daddy." She blushed

"I'm glad I could put a smile on your face."

"You know I deeply care for you, right?" She asked lifting herself off of the floor. She carefully walked to her dresser and grabbed a small piece of paper. I couldn't help but to watch her in awe. Her body was gorgeous. There wasn't a scar of blemish on her body. Her perfectly round ass bounced with every step.

"What's this?" I ask looking at the sheet of paper she just handed me.

"It's my Uncle Donatello. I know you fell off, but if you talk to him you can shake back." She assured. I didn't know it was going to be this easy. I knew all about Donatello. I just couldn't believe she would give it up so soon.

"I thought you…" She kissed my lips before I could finish my sentence.

"You my man, right?" She spoke in between kisses.

"Yeah," I replied grabbing her by her head and forcing my tongue down her throat. I quickly pulled away.

"Is he expecting my call?" I questioned.

"Yes, I told him you were my boyfriend and you got jammed up and lost your connect."

"And what did he say?"

"He'll help you on the strength of me. He just want to chat with you personally first."

"You really came through for a nigga." I expressed as I wrapped my arms around her playfully.

"Look, I'm about to bounce. It's pretty late. I'll call you tomorrow." I stated as I stood to my feet and began to get dressed.

"Okay, bae. I wish I could be up under you all day, but I understand. Remember Mun, do not fuck over my uncle and only you deal with him."

"You talking to a real nigga. You don't have to worry about none of that slick ass shit going down. Believe that." I assured her angrily as I grabbed my car keys off the dresser. I don't know what type of nigga Danielle think I am, but she really insulted me with her last comment. Before I say something I'll regret, I kissed her on the forehead and left.

CHAPTER 48
BRE

I know this motherfucka see me calling that damn phone, I thought as I sat on the edge of the bed beyond frustrated. It's 1:20 a.m. He left the house over ten hours ago. This not even like Mun. I know he has a lot of catching up to do, but damn. He always answers his phone. I finally grew tired of hearing the white lady on his answer machine. I tossed my phone behind me onto my bed and headed towards the restroom.

"I can't believe this nigga," I thought out loud, removing my clothes. I stopped in my tracks when I noticed Mun's jeans lying next to the dirty laundry basket, which seemed out of place to me since they were the same jeans he wore home from the county jail. I reached down to pick up the jeans and toss them into the basket when a small sheet of paper came tumbling out of one of the pockets. I bent down to retrieve the sheet of paper.

"Danielle?" I asked myself with a puzzled expression on my face as I swiftly rose to my feet dashing across the room to get my phone. My adrenaline was rushing which caused my hands to shake tremendously. I could barely hold on to my phone. I couldn't wait to get this bitch on my line. The phone rang a few times before someone picked up.

"Hello." The female answered.

"Is this Danielle?" I asked looking down at the crumbled sheet of paper in my hand.

"Yes, who is this? Who wants to know?" She asked with attitude.

"I'm Mun's wife. I'm trying to figure out why is your number in his pants pocket?"

"Why didn't you ask him? That's your man, right?" She retorted.

"You right. You just another one of his side pieces. You can keep waking up in the wee hours of the night to let him out your house, but just know this where home at." I spoke calmly before hanging up. I can't believe this shit. Niggas ain't shit! I ranted out loud. I held his ass down every step of the way and this is how he repays me. I've been nothing but good to his dirty dick ass. Before long, my rampage turned into sobs as I lay on top of my silk sheets in a fetal position before drifting off to sleep.

I awoke to the sound of the shower running. As I looked around the room at the fog on the mirrors from the hot steam, I began to recap last night events. I must have fell asleep waiting on Mun. I leaped out of bed. I could smell the fresh aroma of Irish Spring as I stood on the other side of the door contemplating my choice of words. I peeked my head inside of the restroom and instantly noticed Mun's wet body. The water that ran down his chest looked so inducing and this tingling sensation shot through my pussy at the sight of him. I instantly forgot why I was even upset in the first place.

"Shit!" Mun yelled as he jumped at the sight of me.

"You can't be sneaking up on a nigga like that," He joked as he reached down to wash his lower abdomen. His dick was long bulky and thick and I almost exploded just thinking about him inside of me.

"So, what you got planned today?" I questioned stepping completely inside of the bathroom.

"I got to link up with this new connect." He stated turning off the shower. His dick hung freely as he walked to the sink to grab his towel. Thoughts of him fucking Danielle immediately impaled my mind and I instantly became disgusted. I slowly turned to walk away and was stopped by Mun's grip as he held my wrist.

"Where you going? He asked standing in front of me. His body was so close to mine. I could feel his breath.

"Muni m—"

I couldn't even finish my sentence before I was interrupted by the sound of the doorbell. I snatched my arm away from Mun's grasp and headed to the door. I just needed to get away from him before I blow up and do or say something I'll regret. It has always been an issue for me to bite my tongue when it's something on my chest. I stood on the tip of my toes and peeped through the peephole. Donk and Kadejah stood on the front step.

"Hey y'all." I greeted them blissfully as I stood to the side and let them inside. Kadejah bypassed me and ran straight to the back.

"You good?" Donk ask nonchalantly without even looking my way. Ashamed, I nodded and quickly exited the room. Only to bump into Kadejah running down the hallway.

"Hey mommy. Come on Uncle Donk, the toys this way!" She yelled quickly dismissing my presence as she tugged on Donk's Gucci Letterman jacket.

"I'll play with you later, baby girl. Me and your Uncle Mun have to go handle some business. Okay?" He asked hovering over her small body. Kadejah lowered her head in disappointment.

"You promise?" She asked with a piteous expression on her face. Donk reached down and held Kadejah's head up.

"Never fear—"

"I'm here." She joined in finishing off his sentence. He planted a kiss on her forehead.

"You ready?" Mun ask Donk while standing next to me. His Jimmy Choo cologne instantly filled my nostrils as I eyed him closely.

"Yeah" Donk replied walking toward the door. Mun leaned in and planted a soft wet kiss on my lips.

"I love you too." I mumbled keeping my eyes trained on Kadejah. I didn't want Kadejah to feel the uneasy vibe between Mun and I. He knelt down and joked with Kadejah before marching out of the house. I instantly regretted treating him so nonessential. I looked over my shoulders at Kadejah and smiled at the brilliant idea that just came to mind. I figure it was time to make little Ms. Danielle jealous. I darted to the bedroom to retrieve my phone and hurried back to the front room where Kadejah stood looking devastated.

"You want to take pictures with mommy?" I asked Kadejah yanking her towards me. She didn't seem too amused, but she didn't bicker or cry neither. Several minutes passed and I began to send the selfies of me and Kadejah to Miss Danielle's phone. With every picture I inscribed a scurrilous text. I laughed hysterically as I mentally devised other devious things. I refused to let a bitch take my man.

Hours later, Kadejah and I lay on the sofa as we watched a series of cartoons. My screen on my phone lights up. I open the message from Danielle and what it states causes me to gasp for air.

CHAPTER 49
DONK

Mun and I sit parked outside of Donatello's Restaurant. Not knowing what to expect, I text Lil Tim with the address to inform him to be somewhere in the area just in case some shit go down.

"So, where you meet this cat?" I questioned checking the clip in my 9mm Beretta.

"The medical nurse I was fucking with in the county. It's her uncle. She put in a good word for me." He explained paying very close attention to the pedestrians and the cars that drove pass.

"Oh okay, that's what's up. You ready to do this?" I ask.

"Yeah," he replied.

Even though the deal was for Mun to come alone, I convinced him otherwise. We walked into the restaurant where we were expecting to meet Donatello. The place smelled like onions and garlic. We stood out like immigrants among the people who were already seated inside the restaurant. A chubby black dude approached us with menus in his hand. Me and Mun looked at each other with puzzled expressions. The chubby Italian must have picked up on our uneasiness as he raised the menu's to barely cover his mouth.

"Follow me." He mumbled looking around cautiously. As long as I've stayed in Dallas, I never been to this place. Soft music played at a low tune, chandeliers hung from the ceiling and famous portraits and expensive art decorated the walls. It was beautiful. We walked through a door that separated us from the restaurant which led to the basement. Once inside, a bulky Mexican guy blocked the entrance to another door. I'm assuming that's where all the business took place. He carried an AR-15 on his shoulder and his black shades covered his eyes. I wasn't moved a bit. Regardless of the situation, I'm gone die bussing. Never knees in the dirt. The chubby Italian stepped aside and whispered something to the guy in front of the door.

"Gentlemen, no weapons are allowed past this point." The chubby Italian directed. Mun and I looked at each other. It was all or nothing.

"You still sure about this?" I asked Mun feeling a bit uneasy. This could be a set up or anything, I wasn't too sure about this shit.

"Fuck it, it is what it is." Mun replied lifting his shirt and removing his 40 Cal. He glanced at me and shrugged. I knew for him to remove his piece, he must have really needed to speak with Donatello.

"If you with it, I'm with it." I chanted before lifting the bottom of my jeans, removing my 38 Special, and the 357 Magnum that was tucked inside of my waist. I began to fix my clothing and smooth out my wrinkles ready to meet the guy on the other side of the door. I noticed Mun glaring at me.

I let out an irritated sigh before reaching behind and retrieving the 9mm Beretta from my back side.

"Are you done?" The chubby bald dude asked arrogantly. He looked over at the Mexican guy and gave him the cue. One by one, he thoroughly patted Mun and I. When he finished, he knocked on the door to alert whoever was on the other side. Then,, he opened it wide enough for us to enter. Once inside, I didn't utter a word. I just scanned the room to see how many people Mun and I were up against if it came to that point. The lights were slightly dimmed but I could see the two men sitting at the table portraying as if they were playing poker. Cards and poker chips lay spread out across the table and a half bottle of Hennessey. Weed smoke filled the air and I'm not talking about the regular backyard bullshit.

"You prefer to sit or stand?" One of the dudes asked. I was assuming he was Donatello.

"We'll stand." I answered quickly.

"Which one is Mun?" He questioned as he stood to his feet. What Mun didn't know was I had Persuasia's burner on me. She called it her prostitute pistol. A two-shot revolver and it was tiny, so small it barely covered the palm of your hand. I already mentally mapped out how shit would play out, but if push comes to shove me and my nigga gon' make it out this bitch.

"I'm Mun." He stated taking a step forward.

"My niece tells me nothing but great things about you, and I would gladly assist you since it will be benefiting her as well." He suggested. Donatello looked to be in his mid-fifties. His salt and pepper facial hair was neatly trimmed and his ponytail hung to the middle or his back. He was dressed in all black suit, but his thick rings and gold bracelet is what really caught my eye. He looked no less than two hundred pounds, but I had a feeling he did more than smoke weed.

"What's the tag on a brick of powder cocaine?" Mun asked.

"I understand you took a loss. If you cop five or more, I'll give them to you for fifteen a pop, but after a few months it will go back to the regular price, which is eighteen." I swallowed the lump in my throat avoiding eye contact with Mun to hide the excitement. Business was going to be lovely from now on.

"Okay, bet. You got a sample of what I'm buying?" Mun asked Donatello who turned and looked at the dude who sat across from him at the table. He reached into a small compartment under the table and tossed a small bag to Donatello. Donatello carefully opened the bag and handed it to Mun. Mun dipped his finger into the bag and twirled it around his mouth so he can determine just how pure the Coke was. I could tell by the sour look on Mun's face that the shit was grade A.

"I want ten." Mun instantly requested.

"Okay, tomorrow at 6 pm. We'll meet up. Bring the 150,000. Nothing less. I'll text you with the address later." He said sealing the deal with a firm handshake. "Take care of my niece." He stated as Mun and I headed out the door.

"She's in good hands." Mun responded sounding like the dude from the Allstate commercial. I was so relieved once I tucked my burner back into my jeans. With the prices we getting, we were sure to flood the streets.

Ah'Million

CHAPTER 50
MUN

I knew purchasing the ten keys would most definitely put a dent in my pocket. I got twenty from Lil Tim, which surprised me he had that much. I was really starting to view him different. He wasn't the ordinary young nigga. Donk hit me off with fifty, which made the rest a lot easier to come off. It was time to get to this money while these prices low. After Donk and I rapped with Lil Tim, we headed back to my crib. I already knew Donk would be in and out since Persuasia had been blowing up his phone since the meeting with Donatello. We stepped into the house. I could smell Bre's food from the porch. Kadejah greeted us both with kisses and hugs like always. I walked into the kitchen behind Bre and wrapped my arms around her waist.

"You missed me?" I teased nibbling at her earlobe.

"Of course," she stated before turning around to face me. I stuck my tongue down her throat and we began to kiss passionately. Low moans escaped her mouth as our tongues intertwined. A sudden knock at the door startled the both of us.

"You want me to get it?" Donk yelled from the front room.

"Yeah, go ahead." I assured looking at Bre's confused. I headed toward the front room. When Donk opened the door, two women and two uniformed police officers quickly stepped inside.

"What's the problem?" We all spoke in unison.

"We're here to take Kadejah Turner upon a call we received pertaining to drugs and criminal activity. You'll receive a court date which you'll be given the opportunity to prove fit and if so she'll be returned into your custody immediately. If not, we will push for full custody." The CPS lady announced while moving to the side. One of the policemen walked towards Kadejah and picked her up placing her on his shoulder.

"Hold the fuck up!" Donk yelled snatching Kadejah away from the officer. The other policeman drew his weapon and I swiftly stepped in between the officer and Donk.

"Now, you know you all the way out of line for drawing that gun in front of a child. It's no one in here armed." I stated holding both my hands out. I looked over at Donk who was breathing heavy as he mugged the officers with Kadejah on his waist. Bre was sobbing uncontrollably and my head begin to spin.

"Who sent you ma'am?" I pleaded. I couldn't believe someone would be so dirty and bring harm to a child.

"I can't reveal to you that information but I can set you a court date pronto."

Boom!

I turned around to see Donk tightening his wounded fist after punching a hole into the wall. Donk was furious and I know he wasn't trying to hear any of this bullshit.

"Y'all can't take my little girl. This has to be a misunderstanding. I screamed as saliva flew from my mouth while my veins protruded from my neck.

Kadejah was all we had left. I can't just let them take her.

"Look fellas, hand over the little girl. If not, I'll call backup and you will be taken into custody as well." The police officer announced resting his hand on his weapon. I never felt so defeated.

"Take me! She not leaving my hands homie!" Donk yelled. I got to calm this nigga down before shit get out of hand

"Donk." I called out turning my attention towards him

"Yeah," he replied not losing eye contact with policemen.

"Give her to them. We already know it's some fraud shit in the game. We gon' get her back, believe that." I assured him. He looked me in my eyes. I could tell it was killing him to let Kadejah go. Hell, I didn't want to give her up neither. A tear formed in his eyes and it was no mistaking, he was hurt.

"What's wrong Uncle Donk? Why you carrying her?" Kadejah asked rubbing the side of Donk's face. Donk slowly placed Kadejah on the floor and knelt down in front of here.

"Look baby girl, somebody hating and you gon' be gone for a few days, but I promise you I'm coming to get you." He assured her as she looked around confused.

"Where I'm going? She asked.

"You going with these ladies but willingly or unwillingly, I promise you, you'll be back soon." I interjected.

"That's on Quay and Rochelle. You gon' see ya uncles in a few days." Donk chimed in pointing his fingers at her chest.

"You promise?" She asked with crocodile tears in her eyes.

"We promise." Donk and I spoke in unison. We took turns saying our goodbyes to Kadejah.

"Bre." I called out. Her eyes were red and swollen and she couldn't stop crying. I stood to my feet to guide her towards Kadejah.

"Kiss Kadejah before she leaves. Stop crying, she'll be back." I said holding Bre by her arm. She heaved continuously while her bottom lip trembled.

"I love you baby." Bre spoke through tears as she knelt down and pecked Kadejah on her forehead wrapping her arms around her tiny body tightly.

"I love you too, mommy." Kadejah shot back as she wrapped her arms around Bre's neck. When Bre stood to her feet, I nodded to the officer, giving him the okay to take Kadejah. The officer picked Kadejah up and headed toward the front door.

"Y'all pweese, don't forget to come get me." She cried out as the tears slowly descended down her face. For her to be so young, she took the departure pretty well. We all stood outside until their cars were nowhere in sight.

"Who the fuck would call and report some shit so foul?" Donk asked as he flopped down on the sofa. Me, him and Bre all sat around looking at one another dumbfounded. Several minutes passed and silence filled the room.

"I think I know who did this." Bre uttered with her eyes glued to the floor.

"Who?" Donk and I shot back standing to our feet. Bre then used a couple squares of toilet paper to wipe the snot from her nose, before looking into my eyes.

"The other day I found a number in your pants pocket. The chick was talking shit and it made me very upset. Well earlier

221

today, I figured I'll take pictures of Kadejah and I and send them to her to expose the fact she's just a fuck thang and you have a real family." She spoke through sniffs. I could slap this bitch, I was so pissed.

"So what? What happened after you sent the pics?" I asked aggravated. I can't believe this bitch would drag Kadejah into this shit.

"I'll have that little girl taken away from you and I'll see then if you'll still be laughing."

"Oh, so you knew this shit was bound to happen, and you didn't tell me shit!" I yelled shoving her head so hard it snapped backwards, barely missing the wall behind her.

"You know where that hoe live?" Donk asked grabbing his car keys off the sofa.

"Yeah, come on." I replied walking towards the door, before taking one last look at Bre in disgust. Once me and Donk were out the door, we hopped into his Chrysler 300 and sped off.

"You know I could murk that bullshit ass bitch of yours." Donk taunted as we sat a couple houses down from Danielle's house. The neighborhood was quiet as any other day, but it wasn't going to stop me from waking up this street once I saw Danielle's ass.

"Right about now, I could beat her ass to death with my bare hands, but she's the only way we can get Kadejah back. Both our records are dirty, filled with the exact same shit they claimed they took Kadejah for." I shot back looking in the direction of Danielle's two-story home. I figured it was best if I waited for her to come home rather than call her and the police being able to trace back the call. Donk's phone began to ring and he quickly informed Persuasia on the previous events. I stared out the window as I began to weigh my options. If I kill Danielle that means no more Donatello. Fuck Donatell and fuck the dope. Won't shit stop if I lose him, Danielle should have never gone to this extent.

Several Kush blunts later, there was still no sign of Danielle. Bre been blowing up my phone nonstop since I walked out the door. Yawns escaped my mouth as I struggled hard to keep my eyes open. I looked over at Donk who was still alert as he was earlier.

"Look bro, we gon' come back tomorrow after we meet up with Donatello and set up shop." I insisted. Without responding, Donk slowly pulled off. He hadn't spoken much but I knew with or without me, Danielle was good as dead.

The next day Donk and I waited for Donatello to show up. We were supposed to meet at Pumberton Park on the Far East side. The entire ride over here I thought about Quaylo. She loved the East Side. If I had one wish, I'll choose Quay. I missed her so much. I know her and Kadejah would be inseparable. Rochelle would've been ecstatic. All she ever wanted was a grandchild. Life is a bitch. I think back and ponder on things we all should have done and could have done that we didn't do. I shook my head as the tears welled up in my eyes. I quickly blinked them away and focused on the task at hand. Donatello arrived in a burgundy Escalade truck. He parked two spaced left of me, then tapped his horn.

"I'll be back." I told Donk before opening the car door as I reached under the seat and grabbed the brown paper bag.

"You don't want me to go with you? He asked slightly opening his door ready for action. It didn't matter what time of day it was, Donk stayed ready.

"Nah lil bro, this good enough. Just keep ya eyes and ears open." I replied slamming the car door shut. I opened Donatello passenger side door and hopped in.

"That's ten." He assured handing me the bag. I opened the bag and examined the bricks carefully but quickly before handing Donatello the brown paper bag. I noticed he didn't do too much talking during the transaction, and that was a good thing cause believe it or not that's where most niggas fuck up. He slowly thumbed through each stack, before nodding at his driver through the rear view mirror. He extended his arm and we bumped fist as I exited the vehicle. The emptiness of the parking lot made me a bit nervous, but I kept it moving watching my surroundings cautiously. I hate the fact our business would soon come to an end because I really liked the way Donatello conducted his business. I opened the truck and stuffed the bag in the secret compartment. With ten bricks in the truck, Donk and I headed to the spot to link up with Lil Tim to get this shit jumping. Suddenly, the red and blue lights flashing in my rearview mirror startled the shit out of me.

"We got company." I mumbled looking over at Donk who was removing his pistol form his waist.

"I'm not going back, bruh." He stated looking at me earnestly, yet with assurance. I could look in his eyes and tell he meant business.

"So, we gon' shoot our way out this shit?" I stated reaching under my seat belt to grab my .44 Mag. Before I could get a good grip on the handle, the police car sped past me. I quit fumbling with the burner under my seat.

Wheeeww, I thought looking over at Donk who just silently shook his head. I'm glad they were on another mission, cause that shit could've went either way. Whichever way, I was gon' be ready straight up.

CHAPTER 51
DONK

I dropped Mun off at the spot and told him I'll be back shortly. I needed to check on Persuasia. When really Persuasia was the last thing on my mind. I was headed towards Danielle's house. Since they took Kadejah I been mentally and emotionally fucked up. Serious demented issues type of shit. All I can think about is Kadejah's innocence. She had nothing to do with this petty ass shit. She was just caught in the middle of Bre's insecure ass bullshit. The nerve of her to try and get mad over another bitch when she tried to throw herself on me.

After we get Kadejah back, I might still murk that bitch, that's if it's cool with Mun. I missed my lil baby so much. Sometimes I want to break down and cry, when she and Rochelle come to mind. A tear slowly descended down my face from my left eye, as I listened to the Lil Boosie lyrics "When I see your kids face every stack I make. When I think bout' yay when I'm down I pray I be missing you."

I took one last toke from the blunt before putting it out inside the ashtray. I bent the corner onto Danielle's street and parked in the same spot Mun and I sat in the day before. Today, I noticed there was a cherry red BMW parked in the driveway. With no time to waste, I hopped out the car picking up a small rock and tossing it at her car, activating the alarm. The alarm was louder then what I expected, but at his point I didn't give a fuck. I darted back to my car and hopped in driving a little closer to Danielle's house. A few seconds later, Danielle came running outside with her cellphone to her ear. She was gorgeous, but too bad she wasn't important. I cocked back the hammer on my .50 Cal Desert Eagle and fired two shots that hit her in the chest. She instantly grasped for air as she tightly grabbed her chest staggering towards her car. I hopped out my car and walked towards her firing off shots into her body with each step. Her body jerked from each shot and she slowly fell to her knees. I stood over her and sent one last bullet in between her eyes, giving her a third eye. I began to walk away but decided otherwise. I turned around and emptied the rest of the clip hitting her in her face, legs and stomach. The clicking sound of the gun snapped me out of my trance. So many shots consumed her body, you could no longer tell the color of her sundress due to the amount of blood that covered her body.

I quickly ran back to my car leaving Danielle's body riddled with bullets.

I sat in the cozy loveseat in the front room staring at the walls. No music, no TV. No sound whatsoever. Just the sound of the rain splashing against the windows.

"Bae, what time are you coming to bed?" Persuasia asked standing in front of me with her thin night gown on that revealed all of her body parts. Even in the wee hours of the night and no make-up on, just a scarf that covered her head, she was still so beautiful. I really think I've grown to love her, but it was just so hard for me to tell her. I felt like if she don't know then I can convince myself I'm really not in love with her. That means it's no way she can hurt me. The loss of Quaylo and Rochelle really fucked me up and I can't lose no one, let alone another female so close to me.

"Go lay down, I'm good." I responded. I guess she could sense the frustration as she walked behind me and began to gently massage my shoulders. It felt good momentarily, but I still couldn't shake Kadejah from my thoughts. Tomorrow was the big day and if they say anything other than what I want to hear, I'm taking matters into my own hands.

Mun and I waited outside his courtroom bright and early the next morning. Ms. Tellez, an older black lady that worked as a social worker told us it would be better if Bre went inside the courtroom alone. Us tagging along would give them reasons to assume and become skeptical about the type of company around the child. Minutes had passed and I suddenly became nervous as hell. The hallway we sat in almost reminded me of a food stamp office. Families of different races, kids running and screaming but

I managed to tune it all out. I was just so anxious. I wanted to see Kadejah so bad. One of the kids ran past me and stepped on my shoe snapping me back into reality. When I looked at the little boy, I was upset seeing that these Ferragamo's I sported ran me about two grand, but once I looked down at him I instantly felt sorry for him. His hair was dry and shabby. His clothes were discolored and blotchy like they had been passed down from generations. His shoes were scuffed and barely holding together and all I could think about was our days growing up. It wasn't as bad as the little guy that stood before me, but it wasn't too far from it. I remember sitting in the house wishing a few dollars would just fall from the sky. Or running into someone famous that decided to be generous but it never happened that way.

"Keep your head up because the shit you going through now is only making you strong and determined." I stated, digging into my pockets and peeling off four hundred dollar bills. A huge smile spread across the little boy's face and he took off running towards his mother. He was looking back at me over his shoulder.

"Thank you, sir!" He yelled out.

"You know fam, I'm not even mad at Bre. She was doing typical female shit, but what I do know is, soon we get Kadejah back, we gon' take full responsibility of her like we're the ones who signed the adoption papers." Mun assured me while gazing at the courtroom doors.

"Yeah, I'm positive. Kadejah presence will only help me do better and chill on all that reckless shit, and besides, I feel like I'm more attentive. I really do love that little girl, Mun. She's my Quaylo all over again." I expressed.

"Alright, she can come stay with you, but I want her every weekend. I got a lot of love for her too." He responded.

"Bet."

"And if Bre got a problem with any of that, we'll help her get her mind right one way or another. She'll be missing like Danielle."

I interjected. The doors of the courtroom flew open and Bre came walking out with a huge smile on her face.

"She's coming home!" She yelled wrapping her arms around Mun's neck. Words couldn't explain how ecstatic I was. I immediately pulled out my cellphone to share the good news with Persuasia.

"So, what time can we pick her up?" I asked Bre anxiously.

"She'll be waiting inside the office with one of the social workers on the 1st floor. We can get her then." She replied.

We all got to the elevator and headed to the first floor. As soon as the door on the elevator opened, I noticed Kadejah sitting on the bench with her hands tucked underneath her legs as her little feet dangled back and forth. She looked so beautiful.

"Kadejah." I called out. She turned her head and her eyes grew wide as she gasped for air and took off running into my direction. I met her halfway and knelt down as I wrapped my arms around her small body,

"Uncle Donk, I'm so happy to see you. I missed you!" Suddenly, Mun and Bre bent the corner and joined us.

"Hey y'all. I missed y'all so much, Uncle Mun and mommy!" She cried out as she ran to hug them. I walked over to Kadejah as I looked her into her eyes. "I'm not going to ever leave your side again." I assured her.

"You promise?" She asked clutching my hands.

"I promise."

TWO MONTHS LATER

Donk and Kadejah sits across from one another at the table in the small pizza shack on David Street. Ever since Kadejah moved in with Donk and Persuasia, she's grown accustomed to eating at the pizza shack on a daily. Even though it was a family business and a lot of people wasn't aware of its existence, the food was great. As a young boy, Rochelle would bring Mun, Quaylo and Donk to eat there as well. Business was better than it's ever been. Mun, Lil Tim, and Donk had the city on lock. The day Kadejah as released from CPS custody, Donk informed Mun about Danielle's death. Not knowing if Donatello would suspect him, he kept shit cool between them and continued to cop bricks from him up until two weeks ago. Mun realized the sudden change in Donatello's vibe. His questioning on Danielle's whereabouts had become more frequent and intense as well, which made him feel awkward and uneasy. Donk suggested they fall back on meeting with Donatello before they fall into a trap.

Bre and Mun left a few days ago on their vacation to Jamaica. Bre had been planning the vacation for months, so Donk agreed to hold shit down so Mun could relax and be free. He could have canid sex, swim, get loaded and let his nuts hang. Persuasia was almost done with school due to her attending regular hours and extra night classes as well. Donk finally found it in himself to express the way he truly felt.

"Why you not eating, Uncle Donk?" Kadejah asked Donk while sucking the pizza sauce off her fingers.

"I am. I was just thinking about something." Donk replied stuffing the pizza into his mouth. It didn't matter how many napkins he gave her, she still managed to make a mess each and every time. Donk picked up the napkins off the table and gently dabbed the corners of her mouth.

"Unc?" She called out.

"Huh?"

"I'm so glad Uncle Mun and mama was there to save you that day."

"Yea, me too." Donk paused before finishing his sentence. His face contorted as he looked at Kadejah puzzled, yet unmindful as a hundred thoughts came to mind.

"Uncle Mun and who?" He asked again.

"Mama Bwe." she assured.

"Bre was there? He asked confused but livid. Donk's heartbeat became abnormal, and for a second he thought he stopped breathing as he digested the information.

"Yes, Uncle Donk." Kadejah sarcastically replied rolling her eyes as if she was exhausted from repeating herself. Without another word, Donk pulled out his phone and quickly dialed

Mun's number. As Donk waited for Mun to answer, he continued to interrogate Kadejah.

"Where was she that day?"

"She helped me inside Uncle Mun's car and she came to the doctors place to get me too because Uncle Mun said I couldn't stay."

MEANWHILE IN JAMAICA

"Baby, you okay?" Bre yelled out from the other side of the door.

"Yeah, I'm good." Mun mumbled as loud as he could while sweat beads formed across his forehead and low growls escaped his mouth as he strained to release his bowels. The food they ate at the restaurant earlier had really upset his stomach. Five star my ass, he thought while reflecting back on the price and quality of the meal. The sound of Mun's phone ringing startled him. If it was anyone else, he would have just let it ring, but he could tell by the ringtone it was Donk calling him.

"You good?" Donk asked.

"Yeah I'm good." Mun replies calmly.

"Bruh, is Bre around?

"Nah, why what's up?" Mun asks somewhat concerned.

"Look fam, watch that bitch, She's the one that set me up the day I got shot. I have solid evidence."

"Whaattttt?" Mun ask appalled by Donk's statement.

"Say no more." Mun stated before ending the call. He swallowed the lump that formed in his throat. He never knew Bre to be so grimy, but he couldn't deny the fact she exhibited the signs. She held things from him and the shit with Danielle put the icing on the cake. Not to mention, how she would stare at Donk when she thought he wasn't paying attention. Mun never brought it to her attention, because her eyes gave him the answers to any and all of his concerns. He begin looking around for his gun when he remembered he left it underneath his pillow.

I'm gon' just play it cool. She don't even know I know what's going on. Mun thought to himself while wiping his ass and flushing the toilet. He slowly walked to the door and opened it immediately spotting Bre, who sat at the edge of the bed watching TV. As soon as Mun stepped out, Bre spun around and stood to her feet pulling the .44 Magnum from underneath her shirt.

"First it was the hustle, then it was Quaylo and now it's Donk. I gave you all of me, but I'm always second in your life. She stated pointing the gun in his direction. Mun dropped his head in disgust.

"Really, my family, my loved ones? Are you serious?" Mun yelled in disbelief.

"Save the shit. So you can tell your mother and sister about it." A knock at the door caused both of them to divert their attention. Bre scurried across the room, with her eyes trained on Mun as she stood on the tips of her toes to look out the peep hole.

Boom!

The shot from the shotgun rang out as Bre's blood and brain matter splattered all over the walls. Donk had saved him yet again, he thought but his hopes immediately died when he saw Donatello's face.

To Be Continued...
Toe Tag 2
Coming Soon

Submission Guideline

Submit the first three chapters of your completed manuscript to ldpsubmissions@gmail.com, subject line: Your book's title. The manuscript must be in a .doc file and sent as an attachment. Document should be in Times New Roman, double spaced and in size 12 font. Also, provide your synopsis and full contact information. If sending multiple submissions, they must each be in a separate email.

Have a story but no way to send it electronically? You can still submit to LDP/Ca$h Presents. Send in the first three chapters, written or typed, of your completed manuscript to:

LDP: Submissions Dept
Po Box 870494
Mesquite, Tx 75187

DO NOT send original manuscript. Must be a duplicate.

Provide your synopsis and a cover letter containing your full contact information.

Thanks for considering LDP and Ca$h Presents.

BOW DOWN TO MY GANGSTA

By **Ca$h**

TORN BETWEEN TWO

By **Coffee**

BLOOD STAINS OF A SHOTTA **III**

By **Jamaica**

STEADY MOBBIN **III**

By **Marcellus Allen**

BLOOD OF A BOSS **VI**

SHADOWS OF THE GAME II

By **Askari**

LOYAL TO THE GAME **IV**

By **T.J. & Jelissa**

A DOPEBOY'S PRAYER **II**

By **Eddie "Wolf" Lee**

IF LOVING YOU IS WRONG… **III**

By **Jelissa**

TRUE SAVAGE **VII**

MIDNIGHT CARTEL

DOPE BOY MAGIC

By **Chris Green**

BLAST FOR ME **III**

DUFFLE BAG CARTEL **IV**

HEARTLESS GOON **III**

By **Ghost**

A HUSTLER'S DECEIT III

KILL ZONE **II**

BAE BELONGS TO ME III

Ah'Million

SOUL OF A MONSTER III
By **Aryanna**
THE COST OF LOYALTY **III**
By **Kweli**
THE SAVAGE LIFE II
By **J-Blunt**
KING OF NEW YORK V
COKE KINGS IV
BORN HEARTLESS II
By **T.J. Edwards**
GORILLAZ IN THE BAY V
De'Kari
THE STREETS ARE CALLING II
Duquie Wilson
KINGPIN KILLAZ IV
STREET KINGS III
PAID IN BLOOD III
CARTEL KILLAZ III
Hood Rich
SINS OF A HUSTLA II
ASAD
TRIGGADALE III
Elijah R. Freeman
KINGZ OF THE GAME V
Playa Ray
SLAUGHTER GANG IV
RUTHLESS HEART II
By Willie Slaughter
THE HEART OF A SAVAGE II

Toe Tagz

By Jibril Williams

FUK SHYT II

By Blakk Diamond

THE DOPEMAN'S BODYGAURD II

By Tranay Adams

TRAP GOD II

By Troublesome

YAYO II

A SHOOTER'S AMBITION II

By S. Allen

GHOST MOB

Stilloan Robinson

KINGPIN DREAMS

By Paper Boi Rari

CREAM

By Yolanda Moore

SON OF A DOPE FIEND II

By Renta

FOREVER GANGSTA II

By Adrian Dulan

LOYALTY AIN'T PROMISED

By Keith Williams

THE PRICE YOU PAY FOR LOVE

By Destiny Skai

THE LIFE OF A HOOD STAR

By Rashia Wilson

TOE TAGZ II

By Ah'Million

<u>Available Now</u>

RESTRAINING ORDER **I & II**
By **CA$H & Coffee**
LOVE KNOWS NO BOUNDARIES **I II & III**
By **Coffee**
RAISED AS A GOON I, II, III & IV
BRED BY THE SLUMS I, II, III
BLAST FOR ME I & II
ROTTEN TO THE CORE I II III
A BRONX TALE I, II, III
DUFFEL BAG CARTEL I II III
HEARTLESS GOON
A SAVAGE DOPEBOY
HEARTLESS GOON I II
By **Ghost**
LAY IT DOWN **I & II**
LAST OF A DYING BREED
BLOOD STAINS OF A SHOTTA I & II
By **Jamaica**
LOYAL TO THE GAME
LOYAL TO THE GAME II
LOYAL TO THE GAME III
LIFE OF SIN I, II III
By **TJ & Jelissa**
BLOODY COMMAS I & II
SKI MASK CARTEL I II & III
KING OF NEW YORK I II,III IV
RISE TO POWER I II III

COKE KINGS I II III

BORN HEARTLESS

By **T.J. Edwards**

IF LOVING HIM IS WRONG…I & II

LOVE ME EVEN WHEN IT HURTS I II III

By **Jelissa**

WHEN THE STREETS CLAP BACK I & II III

By **Jibril Williams**

A DISTINGUISHED THUG STOLE MY HEART I II & III

LOVE SHOULDN'T HURT I II III IV

RENEGADE BOYS I II III IV

By **Meesha**

A GANGSTER'S CODE I &, II III

A GANGSTER'S SYN I II III

THE SAVAGE LIFE

By J-Blunt

PUSH IT TO THE LIMIT

By **Bre' Hayes**

BLOOD OF A BOSS **I, II, III, IV, V**

SHADOWS OF THE GAME

By **Askari**

THE STREETS BLEED MURDER **I, II & III**

THE HEART OF A GANGSTA I II& III

By **Jerry Jackson**

CUM FOR ME

CUM FOR ME 2

CUM FOR ME 3

CUM FOR ME 4

CUM FOR ME 5

An **LDP Erotica Collaboration**
BRIDE OF A HUSTLA **I II & II**
THE FETTI GIRLS **I, II& III**
CORRUPTED BY A GANGSTA I, II III, IV
BLINDED BY HIS LOVE
By **Destiny Skai**
WHEN A GOOD GIRL GOES BAD
By **Adrienne**
THE COST OF LOYALTY I II
By Kweli
A GANGSTER'S REVENGE **I II III & IV**
THE BOSS MAN'S DAUGHTERS
THE BOSS MAN'S DAUGHTERS II
THE BOSSMAN'S DAUGHTERS III
THE BOSSMAN'S DAUGHTERS IV
THE BOSS MAN'S DAUGHTERS **V**
A SAVAGE LOVE **I & II**
BAE BELONGS TO ME I II
A HUSTLER'S DECEIT I, II, III
WHAT BAD BITCHES DO I, II, III
SOUL OF A MONSTER I II
KILL ZONE
By **Aryanna**
A KINGPIN'S AMBITON
A KINGPIN'S AMBITION **II**
I MURDER FOR THE DOUGH
By **Ambitious**
TRUE SAVAGE
TRUE SAVAGE II

TRUE SAVAGE **III**

TRUE SAVAGE **IV**

TRUE SAVAGE **V**

TRUE SAVAGE **VI**

By **Chris Green**

A DOPEBOY'S PRAYER

By **Eddie "Wolf" Lee**

THE KING CARTEL **I, II & III**

By **Frank Gresham**

THESE NIGGAS AIN'T LOYAL **I, II & III**

By **Nikki Tee**

GANGSTA SHYT **I II &III**

By **CATO**

THE ULTIMATE BETRAYAL

By **Phoenix**

BOSS'N UP **I , II & III**

By **Royal Nicole**

I LOVE YOU TO DEATH

By Destiny J

I RIDE FOR MY HITTA

I STILL RIDE FOR MY HITTA

By **Misty Holt**

LOVE & CHASIN' PAPER

By **Qay Crockett**

TO DIE IN VAIN

SINS OF A HUSTLA

By **ASAD**

BROOKLYN HUSTLAZ

By **Boogsy Morina**

Ah'Million

BROOKLYN ON LOCK I & II
By **Sonovia**
GANGSTA CITY
By **Teddy Duke**
A DRUG KING AND HIS DIAMOND I & II III
A DOPEMAN'S RICHES
HER MAN, MINE'S TOO I, II
CASH MONEY HO'S
By Nicole Goosby
TRAPHOUSE KING **I II & III**
KINGPIN KILLAZ I II III
STREET KINGS I II
PAID IN BLOOD **I II**
CARTEL KILLAZ I II
By **Hood Rich**
LIPSTICK KILLAH **I, II, III**
CRIME OF PASSION I & II
By **Mimi**
STEADY MOBBN' **I, II, III**
By **Marcellus Allen**
WHO SHOT YA **I, II, III**
SON OF A DOPE FIEND
Renta
GORILLAZ IN THE BAY **I II III IV**
DE'KARI
TRIGGADALE I II
Elijah R. Freeman
GOD BLESS THE TRAPPERS I, II, III
THESE SCANDALOUS STREETS I, II, III

Toe Tagz

FEAR MY GANGSTA I, II, III

THESE STREETS DON'T LOVE NOBODY I, II

BURY ME A G I, II, III, IV, V

A GANGSTA'S EMPIRE I, II, III, IV

THE DOPEMAN'S BODYGAURD

Tranay Adams

THE STREETS ARE CALLING

Duquie Wilson

MARRIED TO A BOSS... I II III

By Destiny Skai & Chris Green

KINGZ OF THE GAME I II III IV

Playa Ray

SLAUGHTER GANG I II III

RUTHLESS HEART

By Willie Slaughter

THE HEART OF A SAVAGE

By Jibril Williams

FUK SHYT

By Blakk Diamond

DON'T F#CK WITH MY HEART I II

By Linnea

ADDICTED TO THE DRAMA I II III

By Jamila

YAYO

A SHOOTER'S AMBITION

By S. Allen

TRAP GOD

By Troublesome

FOREVER GANGSTA

Ah'Million

By Adrian Dulan

TOE TAGZ

By Ah'Million

<u>BOOKS BY LDP'S CEO, CA$H</u>

<u>TRUST IN NO MAN</u>
<u>TRUST IN NO MAN 2</u>
<u>TRUST IN NO MAN 3</u>
<u>BONDED BY BLOOD</u>
<u>SHORTY GOT A THUG</u>
<u>THUGS CRY</u>
<u>THUGS CRY 2</u>
<u>THUGS CRY 3</u>
<u>TRUST NO BITCH</u>
<u>TRUST NO BITCH 2</u>
<u>TRUST NO BITCH 3</u>
<u>TIL MY CASKET DROPS</u>
<u>RESTRAINING ORDER</u>
<u>RESTRAINING ORDER 2</u>
<u>IN LOVE WITH A CONVICT</u>

<u>Coming Soon</u>
BONDED BY BLOOD 2
BOW DOWN TO MY GANGSTA

Ah'Million